J. CAMPBELL KERR.

D0582172

People's Friend Annual

Dear Reader,

A WARM welcome to "The People's Friend" Annual 2010! Get your year off to a great start with 21 brand-new complete stories to read, written by a selection of your favourite authors.

For a little light relief, try something from our fantastic selection of "Poems For Life" — a collection of insightful verses about some of the many magical moments we all experience.

For the green-fingered amongst you, we have "Garden Glories", a beautiful collection of inspiring ideas to bring colour and life to your garden.

Last but not least, we have hand-picked some of our most delightful J. Campbell Kerr cover paintings for you to enjoy, accompanied by readers' memories of these very special places.

So sit back, relax and enjoy all the great reading on offer, and remember — lots more heartwarming stories and fascinating features can be found in your weekly "People's Friend", available at your local newsagent's!

The Editor

Complete Stories

p24

J. Campbell Kerr Paintings

p127

010 Contents

p55

p106

Garden Glories!

Poems For Life

p95

Ringing The Changes

NORMALLY, I don't like New Year. And I *particularly* don't like New Year's Eve parties. Christmas? I love Christmas — cards, twinkling trees, snowmen, Rudolph, Bing Crosby, Judy Garland skipping down that yellow brick road with her unusual companions or singing "Have Yourself A Merry Little Christmas" with tears in her eyes, gifts of aftershave and socks, and, of course, mistletoe.

But New Year? I felt about New Year what Scrooge felt about Christmas. I could never see the point of it — another year older, writing the wrong date on cheques for the next two months, holding hands with two strangers while singing "Auld Lang Syne" and all the curious customs and superstitions. I didn't care for any of it *at all* — until last year, when I changed my mind completely.

*　　*　　*　　*

The telephone rang. It was my sister, Julia.

"I hope you'll be coming to us at New Year." She wasn't one to enquire politely about one's health.

"Well, actually," I began tentatively, "I was thinking of just watching a little television and going to bed early with a drop of whisky and hot water." I turned away from the phone and gave a wheezing cough. "I seem to be going down with a bit of a —"

"Nonsense! If you pander to yourself, you will be ill. No, you'll come to us like last year. We need you."

"Now about last year, Julia," I began, determined to be firm. "Your next-door neighbour had me cornered for nearly an hour and —"

"Yes, I know. I'm sorry. Mrs Sowerby told you all about her operation. Not to worry, Geoffrey. She's no longer with us."

"Oh, dear," I said.

"She moved to Spain. A place in the sun, just a couple of weeks ago, so

6

by A.J. Redcliffe.

*Illustration by
Marianne Vinge.*

you'll be quite safe. And," she added, "you can bring that girlfriend of yours. Jade, is it?"

I knew she was fishing.

"Jade and I are no longer an item, as they say," I said coldly. I didn't feel the need to tell her that Jade had announced that she wanted more "champagne" in her life and was escaping to Wales to be with an artist she'd met.

I consoled myself with the thought that I couldn't compete with such glamour, and then found out she was living in Llandudno to be with a painter and decorator called Gaz. But my sister needn't know that.

Julia went on.

"Mother will be here, of course. She says she hardly saw you at Christmas. She says she'll be wearing a pink carnation so you can recognise her more easily."

I knew from where Julia had inherited her gift for sarcasm, and she'd played the ace of trumps, the Parent Card. And so I accepted my sister's invitation to her New Year's Eve party as gracefully as I could.

MY brother-in-law Roger opened the door to me, and as I stepped into the hall, I was greeted by the skirl of bagpipes. Roger wasn't playing them. It was the Regimental Band of the Black Watch. Roger took my coat and then switched off the CD player.

"We like to give each arrival a breath o' bonnie Scotland," he said.

"Yes, I remember," I said. "And here's a *taste* o' bonnie Scotland, Roger." I offered him the bottle I'd brought.

"Well, thank you very much, Geoffrey. That's very nice of you. We all enjoy a wee dram at Hogmanay, don't we?"

Garden Glories!

IT might be a traditional British garden plant, but who can say that lavender doesn't make the most beautiful — and fragrant — display? You might not know it, but Dwarf Lavender Munstead is the most popular lavender for mass planting.

Its grey-green spiky leaves and blue flowers are a summer joy, as its lovely fragrance is released when you brush against the leaves and flowers. You can still enjoy your lavender in the depths of winter, too, as dried lavender flowers keep your linen and clothes sweet smelling. Lavender Munstead is a beautiful dwarf variety, which grows into a compact 40cm shrub. It is ideal in a patio pot or, if planted in line, can create a fantastic, fragrant low screen or border.

Considered by some to be an old favourite, this timeless beauty is set to go on and on!

Now Roger is not Scottish. My sister is not Scottish. They live in the middle of England — but at New Year they like to adopt Scotland and all her customs and pastimes.

It all stemmed from a short holiday they'd had about five years ago at a hotel in Moffat, when they had seemingly stepped into a kind of time warp, a kind of Brigadoon, where the entertainment for the guests was a White Heather Club mixture of country dancing, an ancient Highlander reciting "The Wee Cock Sparra" and singing along to "Campbeltown Loch". I think the next line is "I wish you were whisky . . ." Anyway, they liked to relive their Scottish fantasy each year's end.

I went into the living-room. Julia and I exchanged waves. She was wearing a white flouncy blouse and a plaid skirt. In one corner of the room Jimmy Shand and his band were lively, but not *too* loud, on the music centre. I knew more or less everyone there. There were friends of Julia and Roger, several

cousins, two nieces, an assortment of aunts and uncles . . . and Mother.

"Hello, Mother."

"Geoffrey! How are you, dear?" She patted the seat next to her and I sat down. "Julia tells me you're not seeing that Jade any more. Very sensible. You can do far better."

Can I, I wondered. I changed the subject.

YOU'RE looking very smart, Mother." She was wearing a stylish trouser suit. "I thought Julia might have put you in a corner with a tartan shawl and a bowl of haggis and mashed weans."

She smacked my knee.

"It's haggis and *neeps*. Weans are small children. Don't be sarcastic, dear. There's some beautiful smoked salmon in the kitchen."

I looked round the room.

"Dad not here?" I asked.

"No," Mother replied. "He suspected he had rather a bad cold coming on and thought it best to have a hot toddy and an early night. He didn't want to pass it on, he said."

I nodded in admiration.

"He's very wise."

Julia came bustling over, a glass of whisky in her hand.

"Here you are, Geoffrey. This'll warm you up before you go."

"Thank you," I said, politely ignoring the fact that my sister seemed intent on getting rid of me.

"When you've had it, you'll find the coal, salt, bread and money on the small shovel in the kitchen."

"What?" Then I realised why she needed me there. I was tall, dark*ish* and reasonably handsome, it could be said.

"Oh, no, not again, Julia!" I protested. "Get someone else."

"You're tall and sort of dark. You're not a stranger, although Mother often says you are, but otherwise you fit the bill for first footing."

Mother chimed in.

"And he's not a doctor, a minister of religion or a gravedigger. I believe that's important, too."

I looked round the room desperately. I ruled Roger out. He was neither dark nor fair, just shiny. Then it struck me.

"You're much darker than me, Julia. You do it!"

"It has to be a man, dear," Mother interjected.

"Well, that's terrible in this day and age," I blustered. "What did Emily Pankhurst fight for? There's probably a European law that says that half of first footings should be undertaken by women. And rightly so, in my opinion!"

"Drink your whisky, dear," Mother said soothingly as though speaking to a fractious child. "And wrap up well. It's awfully damp out."

ROGER saw me out of the back door. As I prepared to slip out into the night I grumbled, "This is all superstition, you know, Roger."

"No, no, no," he assured me. "It's all very old and very symbolic. The first-footer brings luck for the year, coal for warmth, bread for food, salt for flavour and money for wealth. By the way, you can keep the fifty pence."

"Thank you. And the coal? What shall I do with that?"

"Ah! Julia bought it specially. Just put it on top of one of the radiators. She has given it a polish. The coal, I mean." He glanced at his watch. "Off you go. There's only a few minutes. Remember to come in the front door."

He handed me my little laden shovel and as he pushed me out into the damp dark, he tried to give me a word of comfort.

"Remember, Geoffrey, custom dictates that you can claim a kiss from every lady in the place."

"But I don't *have* to, do I?" I pleaded, but the door had closed.

I trudged round the corner of the house and stood on the drive waiting to hear the town hall clock strike. It was then that I became aware of another figure, standing just a few yards away in the drive of the house next door. Just a low wall separated us.

It was a man carrying a little shovel. Now, in such circumstances, you have to be sociable. I guessed it was Julia's new neighbour, so I spoke to him.

"Good evening. I see we're on the same mission." I raised my shovel a little.

"And good evening to you," he replied in a strong deep voice. "Aye, it would appear so. The traditions of Hogmanay, eh?"

He was Scottish. I edged a little closer to the low party wall. He was properly Scottish. The man was wearing a kilt, and a genuine sporran, not one of those great silvery, hairy things, but a proper everyday leather sporran.

"You must be my sister's new neighbour," I said. "My sister's Julia Bishop and Roger is her husband."

"Oh, it's your sister, is it? Yes, we've just moved down here, my wife and I and our daughter, Fiona. We've been meaning to pop round, but with one thing and another . . ."

"She'd be delighted to see you," I said, "you and . . ." And as I spoke the curtain of the window behind the Scotsman was pulled back and two ladies looked out. One was nice — and the other was *wonderful*.

MY companion turned and waved to them and they smiled and waved back. I waved, and they waved back and then *she* smiled and I was bewitched. And then I did the most inspired thing I've ever done in my life, just as the town hall clock began the countdown of the quarters to the first stroke of midnight.

"May I suggest something?" I said. "Why don't you step over the wall and go first footing here, and I step over, do the honours at your house and invite your wife and, of course, your daughter over to my sister's for a wee dram?"

To my everlasting delight, he agreed. As the first stroke of midnight rang out he held out his hand.

"My name's Andrew, by the way. A happy New Year to you."

"Geoffrey," I said. "Happy New Year."

As I approached his front door, my heart beating quickly, I saw a shaft of light to my right as my sister's front door opened and then I heard Andrew's fine deep, Scottish voice.

"A guid New Year to ane an' a'. And mony may you see!" Julia would be swooning with delight.

I took a deep breath as the door in front of me opened, and as a girl with honey hair and twinkling eyes smiled at me I looked into the future and I swear someone in my head was singing, "Some enchanted evening, you may see a stranger . . ."

"A happy New Year to everyone here," I said. I was even speaking in poetry. I wondered if she knew what custom dictates . . .

✳   ✳   ✳   ✳

This year, Fiona and I are going up to celebrate Hogmanay with her grandparents, who, funnily enough, live in Moffat. They are obviously anxious to meet the man who is going to marry their granddaughter, and if I'm lucky enough to be asked to go first footing this year, I'll be delighted. ■

11

An Unsuitable Girl

by Alison Carter.

T HE Dacres family didn't approve of Gloria right from the
beginning. She was glamorous, with her blonde hair and bright red
lipstick, her curvaceous figure, her fashionable frocks, her high-
heeled shoes. That was the problem.

"It's not real, of course," Aunt Maisie said to Jimmy's mother soon after
Jimmy had introduced Gloria. "The colour of that hair of hers."

"Of course it isn't," Jimmy's mother replied, "but what can you expect?"

"But Jimmy's smitten."

"He is," Jimmy's mother agreed. "And, bless him, it's not surprising, after
what he's been through. I only want him to be happy."

12

"We all do, Sylvia," Aunt Maisie said, but her tone of voice did not, perhaps, bode well for Gloria.

＊   ＊   ＊   ＊

Jimmy Dacres had met Gloria Purbright less than forty-eight hours after his release from a Japanese POW camp in Borneo. It was 1945. Gloria was a member of an ENSA troupe. She sang, though not brilliantly. She danced, with a certain attractive abandon. But her chief skill was in talking to the men who lined up to see the shows. She was cheerful and funny, and she had a happy knack of making everybody, tired and missing home, feel as though she was there just for him.

Jimmy fell in love with Gloria for all those reasons, and because, of course, she looked fabulous. In truth, Jimmy didn't analyse exactly why he fell in love, but he fell heavily, and he fell fast.

Illustration by Ben Warner.

"A sight for sore eyes," he said to Uncle Harold, the day he and Gloria arrived at the Dacres family home in the East End of London.

It was the first time any of the family had met Gloria. Jimmy opened the door of his little black Austin, and as she was swinging her long legs neatly out, Jimmy turned to Harold with a look of adoration and pride.

"Isn't she just beautiful?"

"I can't deny it," Uncle Harold replied, smiling at Gloria, and glancing at his wife and his sister-in-law, Sylvia.

The silence from Maisie and from Jimmy's mum was almost audible, as they stood side by side, so obviously sisters, their brown woollen coats,

13

sensible shoes and even more sensible hairstyles almost identical.

Maisie took Uncle Harold by the arm and marched him inside the house. He had, she said, "the carving to help with."

*   *   *   *

There was no denying that Gloria and Jimmy paired up unusually quickly. But, as Jimmy told his parents, things happened quickly in those times, and in those places — everybody knew that.

Batu Lintang camp had been liberated by the Australian 9th Division on September 11, 1945. For many at home that autumn, the war was effectively over, but in sweltering Borneo thousands of men, all hungry and many ill, were only just beginning the long journey home.

The arrival of the allied troops had been, to them, almost miraculous. The arrival of a small ENSA troupe, also about to travel homeward but happy to cheer the boys on their way, was almost more miraculous.

Jimmy didn't notice that half of them were amateurs. He didn't care if their costumes, far from new, were suffering badly from the effects of the tropics. He saw only fresh faces, smiles, glamour, a bit of fun, and Gloria Purbright, whose name seemed to fit her so wonderfully.

If he'd thought he had a chance, Jimmy would have proposed to Gloria five minutes after first laying eyes on her, when he hung about outside the flap of canvas the troupe so comically labelled Stage Door. It was a good thing he never told his parents that.

In the event, he didn't have the courage, and he thought it a vain hope anyway — pretty girls didn't agree to marry mosquito-bitten soldiers weighing in at eight stone nine. Not after a few hours of conversation during which they talked about crazy things: their first meal when they got back home, Christmas, childhood toys — anything but the misery and suffering of the past months.

When he rediscovered Gloria two weeks later, reapplying her lipstick as she sat on her tiny, battered suitcase on the deck of the ship home, Jimmy decided that the world was full of miracles. They were engaged before the boat reached Southampton.

Gloria visited Jimmy daily in the military hospital, travelling up and down on the train from her mum and dad's house in Croydon. Thankfully, there was nothing badly wrong with him physically — Jimmy had been a strong and healthy young man when he set off with his regiment — and he recovered well.

After a few weeks he was ready to move into digs in Holborn. The idea was to take up again the training in technical drawing that he'd had to abandon when he went to war. The Dacres family had great plans for Jimmy, in the respectable building firm they owned and ran.

"I've seen a few things, my darling," Jimmy said to Gloria. They were tanding outside the doors of the hospital he'd just left.

"It's been a tricky few years and I've got heartily sick of it. But just looking
t you helps me forget it. Some of it."

He kissed her, and she laughed and took his arm. Her slim-waisted coat
wung attractively. Jimmy thought he'd never seen anything so joyous, so
ife-giving, as Gloria Purbright of the Entertainments National Service
Association.

"Will your parents be all right," he went on, "if I take you home this
weekend to meet my family?"

Gloria looked at him.

"Well, they'll have to be, Jimmy, love, won't they? When we're married
hey'll have to do without me for good!"

It was Jimmy's turn to laugh.

"They will that, my darling. I'm to fetch the keys for my rooms tonight,
and then we're on a train westward!" He slowed his step.

"You mustn't mind them if they're reserved. It's their way. You'll love Mum
and Dad."

But will they love me, Gloria wondered.

JIMMY was no fool. He didn't pretend to his parents, or to Aunt Maisie
and Uncle Harold, that his romance or engagement had been careful, or
measured. The war had driven all pretence out of him. He told his
mother all about Gloria in preparation for their meeting. He was proud that
she was a dancer, and a singer. He talked endlessly about her beauty and her
liveliness.

"The ENSA lot," he told her, "well, they helped in our war. I saw them
before the Japs got us, and then when the Aussies got us out, there they were
again, like a — like an oasis in the desert. They got as hot as us, and as sick,
but they kept going. My Gloria is a sticker, and she's the love of my life,
Mum. I'm looking forward to introducing the two of you."

Jimmy knew that his parents would be as strait-laced when he got home as
they'd been when he left. The war would have changed them a little, he was
sure. They had waited all that agonising time for news, good or bad, of their
beloved only son — only child — after all. Who came through a terrible war
unaltered? But it might take time for them to love Gloria as he did. She
wasn't exactly what you might call, in Dacres terminology, "suitable".

Jimmy's mum, Sylvia, was polite at all times to Gloria. She asked about
her family, and the Far East. But she didn't seem to want too much detail
about the shows.

"I know that ENSA was a vital part of the effort to keep the men's spirits
up," she said. But Jimmy noticed that his particular spirits were not
mentioned.

"Were you always interested in the theatre, Gloria?" Sylvia asked one

Sunday afternoon, when the family were sitting round the fire in a tidy semi
circle, drinking tea from the china that Sylvia reserved for best.

Gloria laughed.

"'Theatre' is a bit of a fancy word for it, Mrs Dacres," she said. "My mum
was a variety performer, and my dad was a booker — he arranged acts for the
halls, mainly on the south coast. So I was always going to be a performer. But
I'm no Lady Macbeth!"

Sylvia's eyebrows lifted visibly.

"In fact, I didn't have time really to turn professional before the war broke
out. I was still at home with my mum till then, but they said I ought to join
the troupe, obviously. Good experience, my dad said."

"Experience, yes," Aunt Maisie said, looking over her half-glasses.
"Experience has its up sides, and its down sides."

Sylvia nodded, and there was a short silence before Jimmy's dad suggested
they put the kettle on again.

J IMMY wanted to talk about their wedding. He wanted to marry Gloria as
soon as possible; what was the point of waiting? Life, he knew very well,
was too short to be wasted in delay.

It was Gloria who slowed him down. The family were spending a Saturday
afternoon on a walk in Epping Forest, an activity that Gloria wasn't well
prepared for, in her glossy high heels and narrow skirt.

"Oh, will you look?" she called to Jimmy, glancing down at one slim leg.
"A great ladder!"

She ran to catch up with him and he put an arm around her.

"Speaking of clothes, and dressing up, and that sort of thing, I —"

"Which we weren't really, were we, Jimmy?" Gloria teased him.

"Nevertheless, when is the big day going to be?" he pressed.

"Oh, Jimmy." Gloria reached up and kissed him. "I would so much like
'do'. Can we save up, just for a little while, like I said?"

Sylvia had walked up beside them.

"You don't think it would be a little . . . ostentatious, Jimmy, spending good
money on a party, when so many are having to go without?" she put in.

Gloria chose to answer Sylvia's question herself.

"I do see that, Mrs Dacres," she said. "But it's my special day, my only
wedding day."

"You'll have to say 'Mum' soon, Gloria," Jimmy said, grinning. "Maybe
you'd better get there gradually via 'Sylvia', eh, Mum?" He turned to his
mother who remained silent.

Gloria smiled weakly and took Jimmy's hand.

"Well, about the wedding, it's just the way I am, I suppose. In my family
we always like a knees-up."

"Yes, I imagine that's your way," Aunt Maisie put in as she caught up on the

16

Glasgow University, Glasgow, Scotland

I'VE had a trip down memory lane thanks to your great cover illustration this week. My son attended Glasgow University, studying medicine, from 1970-77, and I had many occasions to visit him there and wander round this beautiful university.

Its breathtaking architecture always made me stop and stare, and when my son graduated I was quite sad that I wouldn't have a reason to go back again.

My husband joked that he was glad — the car's suspension was never quite the same after all the food and other essentials that we regularly took up to my son in his little flat on Byers Road! I, however, miss my trips to Glasgow, and I will never forget the stunning quadrangles and wonderful atmosphere of that university.

— Mrs D.L., Inverness.

J. CAMPBELL KERR.

footpath. She turned to Sylvia.

"Anyone would think you wanted these two young people to rush into a wedding, Sylvia. And I'm sure you don't."

Jimmy wanted only to make Gloria happy, so he agreed that they would save up, Gloria working in the haberdasher's in Croydon where she'd secured a job, and Jimmy putting away some of what his father paid him for the drawings he was already producing.

They met as often as work and family would allow — in Croydon, at the Dacres', or for precious half-hours together over cups of tea and buns in London.

Jimmy noticed that his mother's clothes, and Aunt Maisie's, seemed to get more sensible each time Gloria visited.

He waited for them to fall for Gloria a little. He loved them both very much, but he knew they felt some disapproval towards his fiancée. Sylvia was a woman of immense kindness, and her sister Maisie, although even more stiff in her manner, was the same.

Dad, and Harold — well, they tended to keep out of the way, visiting building sites, or in their treasured sheds, or on the allotment. They were brothers-in-law and also great friends. They avoided making judgements, Jimmy knew, seeing that their wives had long ago taken on that particular task. But Sylvia and Maisie both prized respectability. Gloria would never fit their mould.

At the beginning, the contrast just made Jimmy laugh inwardly at the way he could love them all so much, coming as they did from opposite ends of some feminine spectrum. Mum and Maisie couldn't help but love Gloria, in time.

Mum needed to get used to having him back anyway. She'd been through such terrible anxiety. She would be ready to share him soon.

"I LONG, long, long for rationing to end," Gloria said one day as the women prepared a meagre Sunday roast, their rations pooled. "I thought I'd come home from the tropics to lamb chops, fresh butter every day and chocolates galore!"

"At least it's made us less wasteful," Maisie said, picking up a sharp knife.

"What we can do in this house with a parsnip," Sylvia commented, smiling at Gloria. "You wouldn't believe!"

"Sorry, Mrs Dacres," Gloria said gaily. "I can't bear parsnips. Never could, never will. I'd rather eat the soil they were dug up from!"

Sylvia, who prided herself on using every ounce of produce that her husband Eddie brought home from his allotment, stared at Gloria.

"And I," Jimmy said, anxious to make peace, "eat what I'm given, as long as nobody tries to feed me rice!"

"It's not an interest of yours, Gloria?" Maisie asked. "Cooking?"

18

Gloria laughed her musical, merry laugh, the laugh that gladdened Jimmy's heart. Her perfectly applied lipstick shone in the stove-light.

"It would be, Mrs Jones, if I could do it. My mum never taught me. She tended to be treading the boards around dinner time, as you know. My dad was a dab hand at the buying of fish suppers. We had a running account on Eastbourne seafront, as I recall!"

"Then it looks as though you'll be fending for yourself, Jimmy, when the two of you set up home."

Sylvia scraped the bottom of the little roasting pan that held the piece of topside. The harsh sound rang around the kitchen.

✳   ✳   ✳   ✳

As time passed, and the little wedding fund grew, Jimmy found he didn't look forward to the days when he would take Gloria home to the East End. Once he even found himself making an excuse.

She had telephoned him at work to arrange to meet at Liverpool Street.

"You looked under the weather on Tuesday, Gloria," he said. "Why don't I just come down to Croydon and we can go down to the Lyons' and chat?"

"I'm all right, Jimmy," she said, a note of reserve in her voice. "I never got that threatened cold, thank goodness."

"Oh, that's good. But anyway, I'm a bit tired. I'll just come and see you for the evening, shall I? It'll save Mum cooking for extra again."

"But your mum loves to cook, Jimmy," Gloria said quietly. "And I gave her my ration book for today, remember?"

Jimmy felt as though things were going awry. Somehow the progress of his love for Gloria, and the smooth running of his family, were not going along at the steady pace he had expected.

THEIR wedding was finally set for the September after he'd come home.

"It's only fitting," Gloria said, laughing, "that a year after you gained your freedom, you lose it again to me!"

"I won't have that sort of comment," he said, smiling but also serious. "Marriage is not the end of freedom. It's the start."

Jimmy was full of hopes, but his unease was growing. Mum was quiet on the subject, but there was so little she seemed to see in his fiancée that she could understand or that pleased her.

Gloria was everything to Jimmy, but he knew that men made mistakes. He'd seen it, especially in men who'd suffered. They didn't stop to think — they wanted happiness and they wanted it now.

"Gloria's a beautiful girl," Sylvia said, when he tried to broach the subject.

"And she loves me, Mum," Jimmy insisted, "as I love her."

"Well, I can't say anything about that, Jimmy," she said, touching his arm, a look of unexpressed emotion on her face. "That's for you to know."

Maisie he could ignore — she was his aunt and he was fond of her, but it was his parents whose views he wanted. Jimmy found his dad one cold early spring day in the shed. Eddie reddened when Jimmy began to talk about Gloria, and about his mother's attitude.

"Oh, now, Jimmy, you know I'm not the man to ask in affairs of the heart. I'm not the most demonstrative bloke in the world."

"You know how I feel about Gloria, though, Dad?"

"Of course, son. She's a ray of sunshine, is Gloria." He picked up a flower pot, as though in need of something to do with his hands. "I think your mother does ponder sometimes about your future. It's a thing about, um, suitability."

His dad seemed immediately to regret the word. Jimmy could hear the echo of it passing between his parents, and between Mum and Maisie.

"I mean, she's delightful, Jimmy. A lovely girl. But I suppose your mum expected someone a bit more . . ." A crack appeared in the pot as he kneaded it in his hands. Then he brightened, finding a way out of the embarrassment.

"It's just that they're so different, Gloria and your mum. Different . . . backgrounds."

Jimmy left the shed and his parents' home almost angry. What right had anyone to question whom he chose for a mate?

But, tired the next day after a long day at work, walking back to his chilly lodgings, Jimmy started to think. Had he been seduced by Gloria's brightness? Her *joie de vivre*? Goodness knows, he had needed it back in Borneo. The camp seemed a million miles away and a million years ago.

IT was a hot week in July when Sylvia missed her son. Maisie was sitting in the kitchen, on her almost daily visit from three streets away. "Jimmy said he'd be here this afternoon — he has a half-day for study, Fridays," Sylvia commented.

Maisie looked up.

"I recall his Gloria saying that she wanted to look at things for the place they'll want to rent. Maybe he's gone with her."

"Jimmy would always let me know," Sylvia said. She put down the iron she was wielding with her usual skill. "But that young woman knows how to divert him, Maisie."

"You're right, Sylvia," her sister agreed.

When they didn't hear from Jimmy at all that week, Eddie telephoned his Holborn landlady.

"She says she hasn't seen Jimmy for a couple of days, but that his young lady has been in and out," Eddie said carefully when he put the phone down.

Sylvia looked at her sister.

"I'm going to pop into town," she said, standing and taking her jacket from

20

Busy, Busy, Busy . . .

AND so, at last, I have retired . . .
Now for the leisure I desired,
Now for those hours of relaxation,
Well-earned rest, recuperation.

No more deadlines to be met,
And time-sheets I can just forget,
No more beavering away
At a keyboard every day.

But Betty phoned, asked if I'd drop
In daily at the hospice shop —
Not as a customer, you see,
A badge with Helper *pinned on me!*

The vicar phoned, checked I'd be there,
Helping at the autumn fair.
"Oh, no, no trouble, none at all,
I'd be so glad to run a stall!"

And Julie phoned me up to say,
"Mum, will you mind the kids today?
You know they love to be with you."
Well, yes, I can't deny that's true . . .

The garden is a mess, and needs
A massive onslaught on the weeds,
I cannot put it off, I know —
Now, where did I put that hoe?

The kids, the fair, the weeds, the shop,
My muscles ache, I'm fit to drop,
I think I know what would be best —
Go back to work to have a rest!
— Deborah Mercer.

Willie Shand.

the back of the door. "I'm just going to see how Jimmy is. He doesn't want to go losing touch with his family," she said as she put it on.

"Gloria's going to be his family soon," Uncle Harold pointed out quietly.

"Be that as it may," Sylvia said stiffly, "I'll be back before supper."

"Have it at ours, Sylvia," Maisie offered. "No trouble."

✴   ✴   ✴   ✴

The scene that greeted Sylvia Dacres when she pushed open the already ajar door of her son's lodgings was not at all what she had expected. After hearing from Gloria about her many eccentric friends, who all seemed as bent on frivolity and fashion as Gloria was, she had had vague visions of drinking, or worse.

Jimmy lay in bed, wrapped in layers of woollen blanket and linen. His throat was swollen. He was having some trouble breathing.

Gloria jerked violently as Sylvia's footsteps sounded on the planking and she swung round.

"Mrs Dacres, I'm so sorry." The young woman's eyes were red. Sylvia had never seen Gloria without her perfect make-up. She looked younger, and even lovelier. But Sylvia didn't understand her apology.

"What is it?" She fell to her knees beside her son. "What's happening?" But by the time her face drew level with her boy's, she knew.

"Diphtheria," she said in a low voice. "Jimmy, darling, Mum's here." She touched his clammy brow.

Jimmy tried to swallow, but the discomfort made him wince, and made Gloria catch her breath.

"I should have told you, Mrs Dacres. I didn't see Jimmy for days — he was working hard." Gloria spoke quickly, her voice cracking. "He said he wanted to keep at it. I should have stopped him working. It was all for my silly wedding. But he's not as strong as he seems, even after all this time." A sob escaped her.

"A doctor?" Sylvia said, looking around the small room as though the action could summon help.

"He left an hour ago," Gloria told her, gesturing towards a dark bottle on the nearby table. "It's . . . oh, I can't remember the name. Something like a 'sulphur', but not quite. He said it's lucky we have the medicine now. There was nothing before the war. It stops the spread."

Sylvia knew the consequences of allowing diphtheria to run its course. It could attack the heart and the nervous system. It had been an ever-present danger for so long.

"I'm sorry," Gloria said again. "I found him here already in a high fever, and I should have told Mrs Poole, the woman who owns the place, to telephone, but I got so caught up with getting the doctor — I just ran, Mrs Dacres, like a fool — and coming back to nurse my Jimmy." She looked at Sylvia with wide eyes.

"I have some experience, Mrs Dacres, whatever people think I . . . am."

"Sylvia," the other woman said, still staring at her son. "My name is Sylvia."

The two women stayed with Jimmy, taking shifts, until the tide of the disease turned. Eddie, Maisie and Harold came, too, bringing fruit and magazines, and standing uselessly around the room for the few moments that Gloria permitted. She was strict about hygiene, ventilation and quiet. The older woman gave way to her, and took her gentle requests as commands.

"GLORIA," Sylvia said one day when Jimmy was sleeping soundly. "I want to speak to you. I know that I wasn't welcoming, when —"

"It's all better," Gloria said, looking at her fiancé as he lay peacefully between spotless sheets, but meaning to describe the whole situation. "Isn't it?"

"But I was wrong, Gloria. Pure and simple. You love Jimmy, and I don't know why I couldn't see that. I had to wait for proof. It was stupid."

"I do love him, Mrs — I mean, Sylvia," Gloria replied. She paused.

"If you had seen Jimmy when he stood outside our stage door, or when he walked on to that ugly hulking boat, perhaps you would have realised. Jimmy was no Clark Gable after his time in the camp, but we got talking . . ." She smiled at the memory.

"We don't know why we found each other. Goodness knows the surroundings weren't auspicious. Perhaps Jimmy liked me for my face, my figure — but I hope it's more than that." She touched his hand.

"Of course it is, Gloria! That's what I should —"

"I know that I love Jimmy," Gloria interrupted, "for — well, for all that he is. Certainly we knew very quickly that we were right for each other. I know that I'm not many mothers' idea of a suitable —"

"No." Sylvia placed a finger on Gloria's lips. "Jimmy is my son. If I thought he could make a poor choice of wife, then I was a fool. He fell in love with you because he saw what sort of person you are. I brought Jimmy up — I taught him to see past the surface, to look for the truth. What was I doing thinking anything else of him?"

Gloria reached across to embrace her future mother-in-law. Then Sylvia sat up straight and smiled.

"And your surface, dear Gloria, is a surface to delight in." She looked down at her crumpled flannel jacket.

"We'll have to go on a trip to the West End, you and I, ready for your wedding. Shopping. You'll be my guide."

"I would like that, Sylvia," Gloria said. "And in the meantime, we have this handsome soldier to attend to."

"Will he always be henpecked?" Sylvia asked.

"I prefer to call it 'fussed over', Sylvia," Gloria said. "And if he's very lucky, he will." ■

Growing Pains

by Sally Wragg.

P LEASE tell me you're
joking, Charlotte!"
The fact that I've used
her full name should
tell my little sister something.

"You're chucking in your
college course to go back-packing
with Gavin? When you're on the
point of exams? And halfway through a two-year course?"

She looks down, arms hugging her waist; unable to look me in the eye.

And no wonder! How could she contemplate such a crazy idea? Honestly,
Charlie's pulled some stunts in her time but this has to be the best so far!

It's a good job our parents are on an extended holiday in California. It
might give me time to talk some kind of sense into her before they get back.

"Even you must realise it doesn't make sense, Charlie."

I force myself to speak quietly, trying to be reasonable, intuition telling me
that if I'm anything else, she'll only storm off.

"Couldn't you put it off . . . forget Gavin a while? Oh, goodness, love . . .
can't Gavin wait?"

I stand back, trying to keep calm, not wanting to let her see how worried I
really am.

Gavin's name has been linked too frequently with hers of late. If only he didn't have such a bad reputation. If only she could have fallen for someone else!

Everyone tells her she deserves better — even me, and I'm the one who always tries to give everyone a fair chance.

Mum and I have both been hoping that if we didn't make a fuss, their relationship would run its natural course.

Charlie's plan is — or should I say, was — to take a business studies course at the local college before joining the business Martyn and I have built up supplying fabrics for window blinds.

Martyn's my husband. He says Charlotte has a natural flair and she'll be a welcome addition to the family firm. I know he's right.

Up till now, Charlie's always said she wants to join us, too.

She looks up now, a familiar stubborn expression settling on her face.

"It's my life. Isn't it up to me what I do next?" she mutters.

"But you were so keen! Why throw everything away now? It doesn't make sense!"

"Gavin . . ."

"Ah, Gavin!"

I hate the sarcastic tone of my voice and wish that I'd kept a rein on my temper, but it's too late now.

Charlie's eyes flash with anger.

"You don't know him!"

25

I concede that she is right. I don't really know him at all — only that he's the youngest of a large and unruly family, so it's not surprising that he seems to be going off the rails a bit.

I soften my voice with an effort and wish desperately that Mum was here. This situation is too tricky for me to know how to handle.

"I know he misses lectures and hangs round with a bad crowd. He always seems to be in trouble! Of course you think you can change him, but . . ."

"I don't want to change him!"

Charlie looks incredulous, as if she can't believe she'd want to change the man she so obviously . . . loves? Does she love him? Dare I ask?

"He's different when he's with me," she mutters defiantly. "All the rest is only bluster. He's sensitive underneath."

"I'm sure he is, but . . ." But am I? My voice trails away. Sensitivity is the last thing I'd attribute to Gavin Hannigan.

I'm furious with him. Wrecking his own life is one thing, but how dare he ruin my little sister's as well?

How can I tell her he's so patently not thinking of her?

"We want to be together," she mutters obstinately, and fixes me with that look I know so well, daring me to disagree.

"We're going to be together," she says. "Gavin says life's for living now . . ."

✳   ✳   ✳   ✳

I really want to make Issy see Gavin from a different angle. He's nowhere near as bad as everyone makes out.

I take a deep breath and try to relax.

I know my big sister loves me and is worried about me.

"Issy, I'm not you," I say slowly. "You've put such expectations in our parents' heads. School, university, your own business! You've made such a success of things, you don't understand how difficult you've made it for me to — to just be me."

"*I've* made things difficult?"

I can see I've confused her. In any case, she could have a point. I have to concede that throughout our childhood, our growing up years, I was the one who made things difficult for her. I was always dogging her footsteps, copying everything she did, wanting to be included in her circle of friends.

Issy's life was the springboard from which I've lived my own. I wonder if she realises how much I look up to her, and how impossible it is for me to live my life the way she lives hers?

The idea of following her into the family business had seemed a natural progression at the time. But now I'm wondering if I actually thought it through.

Have I ever really thought anything through in my life?

I love Gavin — or do I? Aren't I as confused about that as everything else?

College . . . exams . . . little things like what I'm going to do with the rest of my life . . .

Gavin's always found college difficult, too. He wants to get away, and what could be more natural than wanting me with him?

"I'm not even sure I'd be any good at business," I say cautiously, and Issy gives a snort of exasperation.

"It's a bit late to come to that conclusion," she points out reasonably. "Couldn't you have thought that before you started your course? You could have looked around and decided on something else."

She stares at me as something occurs to her.

"Does this mean you won't be coming into business with me? Ever?"

Ever's a long time. Ever's far longer than I ever thought. But she's right to ask. Is that what it means?

If, or rather when, I go away with Gavin, I suppose it'll put paid to a lot of things.

I'm confused, and so is she.

"Do you know what you want, Charlie?" Issy asks me suddenly.

"I want Gavin!"

"Oh, yes, of course . . . Gavin!"

There's a world of scorn in her voice, stinging me into a retort.

"You can talk!" I snap. "Look at the effect Martyn's had on your life. Martyn's changed everything. If it wasn't for him you wouldn't even be here now . . ."

And neither would I. Has she realised that?

"I've no idea what you're talking about!" she retorts defensively. But I know she's lying. She knows exactly what I'm talking about.

"We were going to run away . . ."

"No, we weren't! Don't be ridiculous!" she declares hotly, guilt written all over her face.

"We were, Issy! Cast your mind back!"

We're watching each other warily. The moments pass and a song comes on the radio. It's a familiar tune, from several years ago, back when . . .

I grin sheepishly. Troubles momentarily forgotten, wonderfully, she grins back.

THE kitchen fades, swallowed up in that song, the scene changing miraculously to a warm day in a long-ago spring, stored in our respective memories, a day neither of us, for differing reasons, will ever forget . . .

I'm sitting on a golden and seemingly endless beach, arms wrapped round embarrassingly skinny knees.

I'm at an awkward stage, waiting to "fill out".

I wish I could say I was happy but exams are in front of me, and then a

27

void beyond exams, dependent on my results. How can I be happy with all that uncertainty? I'm not watching the waves crashing in on the shore, but my big sister and Martyn Goodyear, who has his hands on her shoulders, pulling her close, whispering something which is making her frown.

I bristle with irritation — anyone who makes my sister frown is in big trouble. Does she need me to sort him out?

I dig my hands fiercely into the sand. Why am I so possessive? It doesn't look like she needs me — the frown's gone as quickly as it appeared. Her expression warns me that something serious is going on.

Is something going on? Issy and Martyn? He's the last boy I'd have expected to turn her head. He's a serious boy, intense, different in some way from the rest of us who piled into the mini-bus in the early hours of this morning.

Martyn drove, come to think of it. A born leader, naturally taking charge, he appears so much older than everyone else. I concentrate on the rest of the gang, all college students — Issy's friends — and concede that I'm lucky to be here, if only as an afterthought.

Issy's been working too hard. I should have been working hard, but I haven't.

Mum told Issy she had to bring me along today and though she had a moan about it, it was quite good-natured, and she finally gave in.

It's good to have a day out. I'm fifteen; I shouldn't be stuck inside — the world's too big a place. I wonder if these exalted beings from the college feel the same? As if things aren't quite right in the world and, worryingly, might never work out?

I close my eyes, inhaling a mixture of sea air and sun-tan lotion which spins me light years away, and fills me with a sense of longing I don't understand.

I want to run away.

Where did that thought spring from?

*   *   *   *

"Penny for them?" Issy's voice breaks into my thoughts. She's torn herself away from Martyn at last. He hovers, watching her longingly.

"You wouldn't want to know," I mutter uncertainly. My hands dig into the sand again.

"Martyn's sweet on you," I say, wondering why I sound so accusing. "Has he asked you to marry him yet?"

I'm sort of teasing, but possibly I mean it. Some sort of devil's got into me today.

"Don't be silly, Charlie!"

She colours up, looking troubled, throwing herself down on to the sand and wrapping arms round knees that are far prettier than mine.

Have I hit a raw spot? Are they an item or not? She stares out to sea. She

Downpatrick, County Down, Northern Ireland

*W*E *live in Belfast, so Downpatrick is just a short run down the road from us. I love the sheer sense of history the place has, from the beautiful Down Cathedral to the handsome buildings on Irish Street, as well as nearby Insh Abbey and the atmospheric Ballynoe Stone Circle.*

In addition to all this, the fantastic Saint Patrick Centre is worth the journey in and of itself. It always inspires me to read about the exploits of the Irish missionaries in the Dark Ages. As well as having seen the exhibition ourselves, we always take any visitors we're having stay with us there, as it's a lovely place to spend a morning before exploring the rest of beautiful, green County Down.

— Mrs L.C., Belfast.

J. CAMPBELL KERR.

doesn't have to tell me what she's thinking because I already know.

"I like him," she says slowly. "Too much. I never meant to, but . . ."

"So?" I question smilingly, wanting to help. "What's the problem? He obviously likes you, too!"

Issy's gaze is too far out. I persist, determined. Martyn Goodyear likes her, all the boys like her, and now I know she likes him, too.

"So . . . ?" I prompt.

She takes a deep and juddering breath.

"I'm scared," she says, so quietly it doesn't sound like my big sister at all.

My heart thumps. Issy's scared, too?

"Of Martyn?" I sound doubtful and I'm relieved when she shakes her head.

"No, scared of how I feel about him! All sorts of stuff! Where we go from here, feeling like we do . . . This was never planned!"

"What wasn't? Falling in love?" It seems to be what she means, though she's hardly making sense.

She nods her head. But is love supposed to make you feel this way? I'd always thought it would be something wonderful, even if I can't imagine feeling it for any of the boys at school. In fact, I can't imagine feeling like that about anyone — least of all Martyn Goodyear! What does she see in him exactly?

"It's overwhelming. I can't handle things at the moment."

She tries desperately to explain but she can see I don't understand and it troubles her.

"Exams, college . . . What we're going to do now that everything's got so complicated!"

"Issy, I don't like to see you like this!"

This is my big confident sister talking. Does this mean that when I'm her age, I'll feel scared, too? More of what I'm feeling now, only worse? Where Issy leads, I follow. If she doesn't know the way ahead, who does?

"Maybe you should talk to Mum," I suggest hesitantly. Mum's so level-headed and practical. Did Mum ever feel this way, too?

How come I don't want to grow up now, when only half an hour ago I couldn't wait?

"Mum's too old!" Issy laughs, rather bitterly. "And you're far too young."

"Let's run away," I say, hope leaping up in my heart.

At least it makes her laugh. She's my big sister again. I heave an inward sigh of relief.

"Where shall we run to?" she cries, gleefully entering into the spirit of my plan.

"France!" I rejoin. It's as good a place as any, a clever, sophisticated choice. We've been there with Mum and Dad on holidays. We've both done French at school.

If we went to France, I wouldn't have to do my exams, either, and how

30

inviting is that?

"We could get jobs, Issy!" I cry excitedly. "Rent an apartment, set up home. I can do the cooking and stuff!"

I can't, but who cares? My cooking's a family joke. I could easily learn. My imagination's running away with me and I laugh, taking her along with me, making her see how wonderful it might be.

We haven't had so much fun in ages. She's been absorbed in other things — just growing up, I suppose — but just for now we're children again and, for once, I'm the one who's forcing the pace.

I bounce up, desperate to find the nearest boat, but a shadow falls over us.

Martyn smiles, shyly holding out a hand.

"Shall we go for a walk, Issy? We need to talk . . ."

How come, even given my tender years, I knew exactly what it was that Martyn wanted to talk about?

Love, commitment, the sort of soppy, grown-up things of which, seconds before, Issy had been so scared.

It's family history now. Martyn proposing and then, very Martyn-like, suggesting they put the romance on hold at least until after they'd finished exams. Straightforward, sensible Martyn, who always puts Issy first. I know the conversation as if I'd been wandering at their side that day.

"I love you, Issy. You love me, too. What matters more than that?"

It was all right for Martyn to say it to Issy. So what was so different about me and Gavin?

✳   ✳   ✳   ✳

Charlie's remembering, too. My eyes have grown misty. The sun, the sea breeze, the feel of Martyn's hand in mine, making everything that was wrong in my world suddenly fall miraculously into place.

I never thought how Charlie felt at that moment, nor how I left her dangling in mid-air. We were going to run away! Darling Charlie, so intense, so determined her plan was the solution to our problems when it would only have made things worse.

This thought is followed by another, filling me with shame. What I felt and still feel for Martyn — is that what Charlie feels for Gavin, too?

I've been so wrong! I've made assumptions, imagining I knew what was best for my little sister, when how could I possibly have any idea?

"You're running away again," I whisper, understanding at last. I step towards her and we hug each other, a thing we haven't done in a very long time.

"Charlie, if Gavin means so much to you . . ."

She's shaking her head, too much going on behind her solemn gaze.

"I'm not sure he does, Issy."

"But I thought . . ."

"I love him? Oh, I do in a way, Issy. I'm just not sure it's enough." She smiles sadly. "Running off would only hurt, wouldn't it, somewhere down the line?"

"Then why not carry on?"

I'm confused and I can tell she is, too. She's obviously still working things through.

At last, her eyes lock on mine, and something clicks into place.

"It's the course," she answers slowly. "I'm not enjoying it. It's not what I want any more. I've been hiding behind Gavin and all this talk of bunking off. Gavin's simply brought things to a head."

She sighs.

"You know what's really behind it all, Issy? It was you. You did business studies, so . . . well, you know how I used to be?"

She gives a little smile.

"Anything you did . . ."

"You had to do it as well?"

Now I'm beginning to understand. But then something else occurs to me — and it's not a pleasant thought.

"Charlie, I didn't push you into this course, did I?" I ask.

Thankfully, she's shaking her head.

"It was thoughtless. No-one's fault but my own."

She's grown up enough to admit her mistakes.

When did that happen? And right under my nose? She's smiling for real this time.

"I'll talk to my tutor. Perhaps I can change courses, if it's not too late — or take time out until I've worked out exactly what I want."

"You really have grown up!"

"I was bound to get there some time," she says, grinning. ■

Pick A Card...

by Joanna Barnden.

February 14, 2005

"HONESTLY, Mum," Matthew groaned, shoving the card at Ruth, "it's so embarrassing!"

Ruth was finding it hard to hide her smile. She looked down at the card, a painstakingly drawn picture of a boy and a girl holding hands beneath a rainbow. Inside was written *JM 4 MG 4 EVER* inside a big pink heart.

"JM for Matthew Graham for ever. Who is JM?"

"See!" Matthew cried as she read it. "It's so embarrassing. Jenny McCarthy is so uncool."

"I think it's nice to know someone cares," Ruth said lightly.

"Yeah, but not Jenny McCarthy. She's only eight."

Considering this came from a barely nine-year-old boy, Ruth bit her lip to hide her smile.

"She gave it to me right in the middle of the playground — in front of all my mates! Do you have any idea how embarrassing that was?"

He shuddered dramatically.

"Did any of your friends get cards?"

"No. Just me."

He rolled his eyes as if this was the worst possible piece of unfairness and stomped off to his room, returning

Illustration by Gerard Fay.

33

The People's Friend Annual

only to snatch the "embarrassing" card out of his mother's hand.

"In case you put it on the mantelpiece or something awful," he told her darkly. "It would be just like you to show it to Gran or Dad!"

Ruth just smiled.

February 14, 2006

"She did it again, Mum — a stupid card left on my desk for everyone to see. And look at it — it's enormous!"

Matthew drew the card out of his book bag. It was, indeed, large — a full A4 size in brightest pink, with a very artistic pattern of sparkly hearts radiating across it. One or two of the sparkly hearts looked like they were in imminent danger of falling off any minute.

Inside, *JM 4 MG 4 EVER* was written, in rather better handwriting than last year.

"She seems to like you a lot," Ruth said.

The "humph" that Matthew managed as a reply didn't tell her much about his feelings.

"She is a very pretty girl, you know, Matthew." Ruth laid down the card in front of him and noticed that there was a trail of sparkly hearts on her kitchen floor that she'd need to clean up later.

"Jenny McCarthy? Pretty? Rubbish, Mum." But he preened a little nonetheless.

"Well, I think you're very lucky to have an admirer."

"But Mum — she's a girl!"

"You're lucky she can even be bothered with you. One day you won't find this kind of thing embarrassing at all."

"Oh, honestly!"

And he was off, card bumping at his side, dropping sparkly stars all the way up the stairs and into his bedroom.

February 14, 2007

"Yeah!" Matthew said, coming through the door and heading straight for the fridge, leaving a trail of shoes, coat and books in his wake. "I escaped this year! There's no way Jenny could get to me at secondary school."

Ruth just nodded and passed the peanut butter, picking up school shoes at the same time.

"You never know. Maybe she's just gone off you," she suggested lightly.

"I doubt it," he said. "She still follows me around the park all the time." But there was a new uncertainty in his voice.

"Maybe she's found someone else to send a Valentine's card to this year? Someone who likes her back and might actually send her a card?"

"But I do like her. At least, I mean, I don't not like her, not like that. She's OK — for a girl."

34

Matthew looked up at his mum, his forehead creased with sudden concern.

"I guess maybe I have got kind of used to those soppy cards. It feels kind of strange that she hasn't sent me one this year. I was the only one of my friends who ever got a card that wasn't from their mum or gran."

"Well, you'll probably want this, then?"

Ruth produced the envelope from behind her back, delivered, as it had been made, by hand.

Matthew pounced on it and tore it open eagerly, then saw his mum watching and tossed it casually aside. It fell open on the now ubiquitous *JM 4 MG 4 EVER*, beautifully inscribed in a perfect heart shape.

"Yuck! Hearts again."

"It is Valentine's Day, Matt."

"I know and I hate it."

And off he went, his hated card clutched tightly to his boyish chest.

February 14, 2008

"No card, Matt?" Ruth inquired.

"Might have."

"From Jenny again?"

"Might be. Can I have a sandwich?"

"I hear she's enjoying secondary school. Got lots of friends. Her mum works with my friend in the local supermarket."

"I don't know much about her. She's not in my year, remember?"

"No. She's turned into a really pretty girl with all that beautiful hair. I heard that Nick in your year asked her out."

"He did, yeah, but she said no!"

"What's the card like, then?" Ruth suggested casually. "Is she still having a love affair with sparkly stars?"

Matthew produced the card, hiding his pleasure beneath over-long hair and disapproving grunts.

"She's getting good, isn't she?" Ruth pointed out.

She was. It was a much more sophisticated creation this year. Computer graphics had obviously been Jenny's latest artistic phase.

"She's top at art. Mr Robertson says she might be able to do a GCSE early because she's so good," Matthew informed her.

"Really? That's amazing."

So much for not knowing much about her, Ruth thought, smiling to herself.

"So, did you send her one, Matt?"

"One what?"

Ruth rolled her eyes. Honestly, what were boys like?

"A Valentine's card, of course!"

Her son stared incredulously at her.

35

"No way! Valentine's cards are for girls."

And off he went, clutching sandwich and card, for all the world as if one was worth as little as the other.

February 14, 2009

"Is there any chance of a lift to the shops, Mum? I need to go to the precinct on the high street."

"What? Now?" Ruth asked, putting down the boiling kettle.

"Yeah. Now. Can we?"

"Why?"

"No reason."

"Well, if there's no reason, I won't be bothering myself. I'd rather have a cup of coffee and read the newspaper."

Matthew shifted uncomfortably.

"Oh, Mum, don't be like that. I just need to get something."

Ruth looked at him, biting back amusement.

"That's OK. I can take you tomorrow. We can go straight after school and then you can help me with the weekly shop."

"But that'll be too late!"

"Too late for what, Matt?"

"Just a card, OK? Nothing special."

Ruth grinned wickedly then decided to let her squirming son off the hook.

"Come on, then. We've got time before tea if we hurry."

But Matthew was not inclined to hurry. As Ruth trailed behind him, discreetly browsing birthday cards whilst her son agonised, she couldn't help but smile. He was growing up at last.

Finally, after what seemed like ages, he made his choice and went to the till to pay for it. When he returned with the card in a plain brown bag, Ruth wasn't allowed to see, but later he crept downstairs and shuffled around her as she tidied the kitchen.

"What's up, love?"

He was a teenager now, but he still came to his old mum for advice from time to time, for which she was grateful. She turned to find him pink and awkward before her.

"What do I put inside it?" he mumbled eventually.

Ruth wasn't going to tease him this time. She thought of the little stash of Jenny's cards that she'd noticed in his bottom drawer the other day and smiled.

"How about," she suggested eventually, "MG 4 JM 4 EVER?"

His eyes lit up.

"Yeah! 'Course. She'd like that. Thanks, Mum."

And off he went, pen in hand, leaving Ruth with the feeling that, this year, little Jenny McCarthy's card might make it on to the mantelpiece at last. ■

DOLLY unbuttoned her shiny black shoes and kicked them off, dancing around the room to an imaginary band while I unfastened my stockings and rolled them carefully down my legs. I didn't want to risk snagging them when they were so expensive to replace.

"Please tell me you're not going to Charleston all night?" I asked her, although I couldn't help smiling as I looked at her.

She flung herself down on my bed, pink-cheeked and laughing.

Thoroughly Modern Lulu!

by Deborah Tapper.

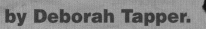

Illustration by
David Axtell.

"I'm in love!"

"Oh, and who is it this time?" I shook the stockings out and laid them over the back of a chair.

"Gilbert? Barrymore? Valentino?" I paused. "Harold Lloyd?"

Dolly squealed in annoyance. She had developed a crush on bespectacled Harold Lloyd when we had seen him dangling from a clock-face about three years ago. A crush that had lasted until the Palace made their twice-weekly programme change and Douglas Fairbanks' dashingly handsome Robin Hood had left everyone swooning in the aisles, my impressionable little sister amongst them.

Only Dolly wasn't so little now. She was seventeen and I was twenty-six, and the nine-year gap yawned like a chasm sometimes, wide enough to swallow us both.

"I shan't tell," she said, sitting up and hugging the pillow. "Oh, Lulu — his eyes, his smile! He's the cat's whiskers!"

"Is he?" I sat down in front of the little mirrored dressing-table and began to brush my hair. I'd had long shining tresses up until a few years ago, when Dolly had persuaded me to get my hair shingled in the modern style. It was at the same time that boring Louise became known as Lulu.

Although Dolly swore the short style suited me, I still wasn't sure about the hair or the frivolous flapper name.

"So where did you meet him?"

Dolly leaned over my shoulder, putting her face next to mine. No-one would have taken us for sisters. I was dark-haired and dark-eyed, inclined to be quiet and serious, whereas Dolly was bubbly and beautiful with her huge blue eyes and dazzling red hair.

AT the Palace," she whispered conspiratorially.

"I knew it!"

We had been going to the Palace for six years, and the visits had become more regular since I had been promoted to assistant floor manager at Blake's and could afford to be a little more lavish with my improved wages. Cheap seats were only 3d and we usually went twice a week — unless the picture starred Valentino or Gilbert or one of Dolly's other crushes, in which case we might see the same programme several times.

Dolly pouted at her reflection in the mirror.

"Oh, no, he's not an actor."

"Who is it, then? Frank in the box office? It's not Mr Pope, is it? You never stop pestering him for stills."

"I do not!" Dolly's blue eyes flashed. "You're a beast, Lulu — and I'm not going to tell you who it is!"

She flounced off and I heard her sorting through our modest record collection, and the rhythmic squeak as she wound the little black picnic gramophone I was slowly paying off at two shillings a week. Then there was a warning hiss from the needle before the lively opening bars of "Don't Bring Lulu" shattered the quiet.

I winced, opened the jar of cold cream and began to smooth it over my face, thinking how different things would have been if our parents had still been alive.

It had been hard, bringing Dolly up by myself. I was only nineteen when the great influenza epidemic of 1919 swept across a country worn down and battered by the war, leaving me and my ten-year-old sister orphans.

I had worked hard, trying to give Dolly the things she should have had, but the first time I took her to the Palace, it was more than just a treat. It was an escape — for both of us.

NEITHER of us had been to see a moving picture before, and I didn't know what to expect as I paid my money to the smartly uniformed boy in the box office. Then we walked down a darkened corridor, Dolly clinging to my hand, pushed through a swinging door, a baize curtain . . . and entered another world.

We sat enthralled through that first programme. The main feature was "Way Down East", and I'll never forget the sight of an unconscious Lillian Gish being swept downriver on a sheet of ice. It shocked and thrilled me in equal parts, and I came out of the Palace with the realisation that life would never be quite the same again.

The Palace's manager, Max Pope, was in the foyer when we arrived, a slim, pleasant-faced man in his early thirties with kind grey eyes and neat brown hair.

"Good afternoon, ladies," he murmured, smiling and nodding to us politely.

He never said very much, but I was intrigued to know the identity of Dolly's mystery love and I suppose I looked at him more sharply than usual, because he coughed and his cheeks flushed red.

"Good afternoon, Maxie," Dolly said.

Poor Max Pope went even redder and looked around helplessly. Luckily for him, the musicians arrived at that moment and he faded into the background.

Jack saw us immediately and whistled, waving a hand, the violin case bumping against his leg.

"Look out, boys — it's Clara Bow and Colleen Moore!"

Dolly simpered and fluffed up her startling red hair, obviously flattered at being "mistaken" for the flame-haired starlet, while I smiled and blushed like a giddy young girl.

Ever since we had bumped into them by accident last month, I had been timing our trips to the Palace to coincide with the musicians' arrival. The trio played during the busiest hours and consisted of sandy-haired Claude, skinny Harry and gorgeous Jack with his deep brown eyes and flirtatious smile. I thought he was devastatingly handsome in his immaculate evening suit and black bow tie, his shining dark hair brushed back from his forehead and his jacket straining across his broad shoulders.

DOLLY wasn't the only one who had fallen in love at the Palace.

"We're playing at a dance next Saturday night," Jack said. "Like to come?"

"We'd love to," I gasped. Dolly was too busy fluttering her eyelashes to answer.

"It's at the Grand — eight o'clock." He winked and turned away.

I gripped Dolly's hand and walked towards Frank's little ticket booth, catching a glimpse of Max Pope's disconsolate face as I passed him.

We reached our seats before the musicians arrived, sitting through the usual disturbance as the elderly pianist gathered up his music and Claude took his place, his companions tuning their instruments with a few unsettling squeals and squeaks. Jack glanced along the front row of seats, but it was too dark to be certain if he'd seen me smiling at him. He shot a quick look at the screen, lifted his bow, muttered something to his companions and launched into a boisterous jazz-inflected march.

Garden Glories!

WE'RE talking very unusual with this stunning Black Bamboo — more correctly known as Phyllostachys Nigra v. Black Bamboo — and often referred to as Oriental Black Bamboo.

Very popular at the moment in both Europe and the USA, this bamboo is rare, dramatic and interesting. It can create a real focus in a garden and has the advantage that it improves each year. As long as your garden is temperate all year round, Black Bamboo should thrive.

The visual appeal of the Black Bamboo is that while the canes turn progressively darker, the leaves always remain bright green, making a very attractive contrast. The stems are green to begin with, change to brown/grey, and then turn black as the year progresses, ending up completely ebony black. This effect is enhanced as the years pass, with the new green stems looking fresh and vibrant beside the jet black stems.

*   *   *   *

Saturday was a million miles away but I was already beginning to worry about what to wear. I laid all my clothes out on the bed and gazed at them in dismay, realising I didn't have a suitable dress. Fashions had changed far too quickly, and the lovely gown I'd made to dance in six years earlier looked so old-fashioned I could have wept.

It was fitted and far too long, swirling around my ankles, while the dazzling

drop-waisted dresses on display in Blake's barely swept the knee. I was thinking about them wistfully as I put my clothes away again. They were all frothy confections in delicate silks and satins or luxuriant brocade, some fringed and covered with countless tiny beads, others trimmed with lace and ribbons or impossibly fluffy clouds of dyed marabou and ostrich feathers.

They were also absurdly expensive. For a fleeting moment I thought about borrowing one of those fabulous dresses, wearing it for the dance and then smuggling it back, but I pushed the idea away almost immediately.

Someone was bound to find out, and I couldn't afford to jeopardise my position at the store for the sake of a dress, not even to impress the man of my dreams.

I picked up the old dress, stroking the smooth fabric as I remembered how I'd thought it would change my life. It was modelled on a Blake's gown I'd fallen in love with when Dolly and I started to visit the Palace, and I'd worked long hours to afford the expensive fabric. I'd worked even longer hours cutting and stitching the pieces together in every spare moment I had.

Dolly — then aged eleven — had been wildly jealous when it was finished, and I had had to make her a matching dress from the leftover scraps of satin. Even at that age, she could see how well the deep rich green suited her pale creamy complexion and flaming hair, and she wore the dress every weekend until she grew out of it a year later.

My dress remained in the wardrobe — a pointless extravagance. No young men came to take me out to dances, as I'd foolishly imagined they would once I had that dress.

I was too quiet and shy, and the few men who had been interested melted away when they found I had a young sister to look after. I spread the

41

beautiful dress out on my bed and examined it carefully. It would be a shame to undo all my previous work, but I was fairly sure that if I let the waist out, raised the hemline and trimmed it with a few scraps of ribbon and beads, I could convert my gorgeous gown into a passable imitation of one of those fashionable new dresses at Blake's.

After Dolly had gone to bed, I took the green satin out again, turned the gaslight up and opened my sewing box.

I worked on the dress all that week, and when I finally put my needle away on Thursday, the respectable gown had been transformed into something that wouldn't have looked out of place on any of the flapper sirens that regularly stalked across the screen at the Palace. I tried it on and pirouetted in front of the mirror, smiling at myself.

I hardly recognised myself as Lulu smiled back at me, all short hair and short skirt, looking as if she was ready to Charleston the night away.

*   *   *   *

When I got in after work on Saturday and dashed upstairs to change, Dolly was nowhere to be seen.

"Dolly?" I called as I took my shoes off and changed out of the smart grey wool dress I wore at Blake's. "Hurry up — the dance starts in under an hour!"

I pulled the wardrobe door open and just stared.

The dress had gone. The dress I had spent every night that week working on had gone. The dress I had wiped out my savings to buy ribbons and green beads for was gone!

I searched through the other clothes on the rail, not wanting to believe it, but there was no flash of dark green satin amongst the plain fabrics.

"Dolly?" I looked into my sister's tiny bedroom. Her work clothes were strewn carelessly across the bed, and after a moment's hesitation I opened her wardrobe door. All her clothes were there, including her party dress — the only things missing were her shiny black button-over shoes.

I sat down on the bed and stared at the wall as the truth hit me. My little sister had taken my beautiful satin dress; the dress I had spent so much time and effort on, the dress that was going to turn Jack's handsome head.

I was numb, then furious, and then I cried.

There was no way I could go to the dance now. I dried my tears, tidied Dolly's clothes away and then, because I couldn't think of anything else to do, I got dressed again, redid my hair and make-up, and went to the Palace.

Max Pope sidled out of the shadows as soon as I walked into the foyer, almost as though he had been waiting for me.

"Hello," he said, smiling at me shyly. "I didn't expect to see you here tonight."

I looked deep into those kind grey eyes and, to my horror, the tears started again.

"Don't cry — please!" Max looked alarmed.

42

He put a sympathetic arm around my shoulders, steered me though a door on the left and into a little room I guessed must be his office. He pulled out a chair, sat me down and produced a clean white handkerchief from his jacket pocket.

"Thank you." I took it and wiped my eyes. "I didn't mean to cry, but it's my sister Dolly . . . I could just strangle her!"

"What's she done now?"

I shook my head.

"She took the dress I was going to wear to the dance."

He gazed at me, clearly mystified by the complexity of female fashion.

"What's wrong with the one you're wearing?"

"It's too long and too plain!" I couldn't help it, I started to cry again.

"I think it's very pretty," Max said gallantly. "Just like you."

That stopped me sniffling.

"What?"

He had gone very red.

"I'm sorry," he said, looking down at the floor and twisting his hands together. "I shouldn't have said that."

"Do you really think I'm pretty?"

"I think you're beautiful," he said softly. "Even more so now than the very first time I saw you walk into the Palace."

I had never heard the normally shy Max say so much at once and I looked at him in surprise.

"I'll get you a glass of water," he mumbled, and bolted out of the room.

I LOOKED around while he was gone, taking in his small office in an attempt to learn more about him. There wasn't much of interest — just papers, old programmes and a few pens.

There was, however, a photograph sitting on the old desk that caught my eye. It was a studio picture; a young couple on a bench against a painted backdrop of trees and sky, holding hands and gazing into each other's eyes. The girl was dimpled and pretty, about Dolly's age, and the boy in the smart Army uniform didn't look much older.

Eleanor and Max, it said on the back: *1914*.

Max came back and caught me looking at it.

"We were childhood sweethearts," he said, handing me the glass and taking the photograph. "We were going to get married when I came back from France, but she didn't wait for me. She broke my heart."

He gave an awkward little laugh and put the photograph away, pushing the drawer of the desk closed.

"I'm sorry. I didn't mean to sound so self-pitying."

"I think it's rather romantic and very sad."

His lips quirked in a rueful smile.

"It would be if it was the plot of a picture," he said. "Valentino would pine for about half a reel or so, but when the true love of his life came walking through the doors of the Palace, he'd have the confidence to go straight up to her and tell her exactly how he felt. He wouldn't spend the next three reels loving her from a distance and hoping she might notice him before the end credits."

"And what would happen if she did notice him?" I asked. "Would the picture have a happy ending?"

"I think so." His grey eyes met mine steadily. "If you're not going to the dance, would you like to watch the programme with me?"

I opened my mouth to remind him that I had already seen it, then changed my mind and smiled instead.

"I'd love to, Mr Pope."

"Max," he corrected me.

"Louise," I said, feeling very daring. "Or Lulu, if you prefer."

LULU," he repeated softly, and the silly flapper name sounded warm and intimate the way he said it. He offered me his arm and we walked past Frank, down the corridor, through the swing door and baize curtain and into the dark auditorium, where the elderly pianist was hammering at the keys with gusto as we took our seats.

It felt right when Max sneaked his hand into mine during the two-reel comedy and equally natural for me to lay my head against his shoulder during the main feature — Lillian Gish again, fragile and delicate in "La Boheme". When Max slipped his arm around me before the picture ended, I forgot all about Dolly, satin dresses and handsome musicians.

We stayed until the Palace was due to close for the night and Max walked me home. He stopped on the doorstep, took both my hands in his warm, firm grip and asked if he could see me again.

"Perhaps I could take you dancing," he said. "To make up for tonight."

I smiled up at him. He wasn't Gilbert or Valentino but I loved his gentleness and his tender smile, and when I gazed into his twinkling grey eyes I felt my heart beat faster.

"I'd like that," I said.

"And, Lulu could I . . . I mean, do you think I may . . ." He hesitated, plucking up his courage. "Would you mind very much if I kissed you?"

"I wouldn't mind at all," I said.

And I didn't mind, not even when he kissed me twice.

*　　*　　*　　*

Dolly was tucked up in bed when I got in and the green satin dress was back on its hanger in my wardrobe. I went into her room and sat on the bed.

"How was the dance?" I asked, a lot of my earlier anger gone now that Max

44

Willie Shand.

Song Of The Swan

THIS is my haunt — where the river runs slowly,
Where light turns the ripples to stars as I pass.
I see as I look in the mirror before me
Another white swan reflect in the glass.
Soft are the waters, unruffled and dreaming,
Softly they slip through the shades of the vale,
And I float like a breath that is lost in the ocean,
Like a ship of white feather with silvery sail.

My song is a song of sunlight and shadow,
Though silent with magic and mystery I glide.
The wind is my lover, it gently caresses,
And carries me trembling home as its bride.
I've plumage like blossom and white wings that shine:
Surely there's no greater beauty than mine!

— Dawn Lawrence.

45

had kissed me. How could I be angry with Dolly when I was so happy at the way the evening had turned out?

She sat up and I could see that she had been crying.

"He didn't even look at me!" she wailed. "Oh, Lulu, she was so glamorous and sophisticated, I felt like a silly little girl next to her!"

"Next to who?"

"Claude's latest girlfriend!"

"Claude?" I was getting more puzzled by the second.

THE pianist at the Palace — the handsome one with the sandy hair." Fresh tears coursed down her red cheeks. "Harry and Jack have a different girl on their arms every week, but I thought Claude was different."

I gathered my little sister in my arms, knowing that if she hadn't borrowed my dress I would have made a fool of myself at the dance, instead of discovering that my leading man had been right in front of me all the time.

"I'm so sorry I took your dress, Lulu," Dolly said, her face pressed against my shoulder. "It was unforgivable of me, but it looked so pretty and I wanted Claude to notice me so badly."

"It doesn't matter about the dress," I told her. "You can keep it if you like; the colour suits you much better than it does me."

I stroked her bright hair and kissed the top of her bent head.

"Why not wear it to the next dance and dazzle everyone?"

"The next dance? Lulu, I'll never dance again!"

"Of course you will. There'll be dances and parties and laughter, and so many handsome young men you won't know which one to choose."

"But none of them will be Claude," she said stubbornly. "What a fool I've made of myself over him. I even took your beautiful dress . . ."

"Forget about the dress and forget about Claude," I said. "When the right man comes along, you'll fall in love and he'll be a distant memory."

She blinked the tears away.

"How will I know that he's the right man?"

I thought of sweet, shy Max and knew exactly what to say to her.

"When he holds you and kisses you and looks at you in that certain way, you'll know he's the one. He'll tell you you're the most wonderful girl in the whole wide world, and when he puts his strong arms round you and you gaze deep into his loving eyes, you'll feel just like the heroine of a moving picture."

Dolly stared at me with a mixture of surprise and delight.

"You're in love!" she cried. "Who is he, Lulu? Do I know him? Where did you meet?"

I just smiled.

"At the Palace," I said happily, and I realised at that moment that the wonderful moving picture house really had changed my life after all! ■

A Heavenly Host

T HE chapel door stood open in the late spring sunshine. From inside, the first strains of the little organ could be heard, as Mrs Penny warmed up for the service. Albert, the verger, was at his station by the door, the hymn books organised into neat piles, ready to be handed out with the notice sheets.

As usual, he was there early, although he never quite managed to be

by Rebecca L. Kershaw.

Illustration by
William Webb.

47

first. Always beaten to it by Harriet, the minister, he perfectly understood that she needed time to prepare, to check on the list of hymns and to spend a little time in prayer.

It was also a relief when Mrs Penny managed to arrive early enough to have a run through of the hymns for the day, loosen her fingers up and get into the spiritual swing. To be honest, she needed the practice.

The organ playing just hadn't been the same since Bill Fossett retired six months ago. No-one could beat Bill at playing the great traditional hymns. None of those newfangled choruses with Bill! He was a great loss to the chapel, Albert considered, as he awaited the arrival of the first worshippers, a very great loss indeed.

As he scooped up a pile of hymn books his arm was jogged by Daphne, the flower arranger, rushing past with her hands full of dead leaves. She ran outside, thrust the leaves into the wheelie bin and dashed back in, jogging Albert again.

"Steady on! You'll have these books all over the floor." He grabbed the teetering pile of hymn books.

"I'm sorry, Mr Downing. Only the flowers have taken longer than I expected, and I had to get rid of the old leaves. Have I knocked anything over? I'll help pick it up."

She started picking books up, getting them all out of order.

"Leave them to me. You go and deal with your flowers." Albert ushered her away and started to stack the books again, shaking his head.

I F he was honest, Albert had to admit that Daphne flustered him. He never knew quite where he was with her, as she wafted around the chapel with her flowers. Albert prided himself on being a steady, solid sort of chap, who liked things to be organised and orderly. He said what he thought, and expected others to do the same.

Which was why Daphne was so confusing. Her conversations flitted from subject to subject, so that he could never keep up, and she herself was as fluttery as a butterfly among her precious flowers.

When he confessed to Harriet how baffling he found Daphne, she just laughed and said that Daphne actually found him very intimidating and that maybe he could try to be a little more delicate around her.

Now, Albert was many things but delicate was not one of them. He decided he'd never understand fluttery women. His wife, Grace, had been anything but. Grace had been solid — that was the best word he could find to describe her. Solid in appearance, solid in character. Everyone knew where they were with Grace.

When he'd had a couple of sherries, at home after church, waiting for the potatoes to brown, Albert would admit to himself that, with Grace, it had been his turn to be intimidated. Just a little.

He had always admired her, from the minute he'd spied her across the floor of the forty-second Lincolnshire Methodist convention at Mablethorpe. He'd continued to admire her for thirty years and twenty-three days of marriage, until she'd died, almost four years ago. He missed her, his solid, dependable Grace.

She'd always loved the garden, so now Albert made it a point of honour to keep it just as Grace would have liked, with lots and lots of flowers, a profusion of colours all spring and summer long.

Albert liked nothing better than to see a garden full of flowers. That was another of his difficulties with Daphne and her flower arranging. She was for ever cutting stems and filling bowls with blossoms which would have been much better living out their lives in the beds around the chapel.

He had suggested to Harriet that they should stop sacrificing flowers on the altar every Sunday, but it had not been well received.

"The congregation likes to see flowers, Albert. They brighten up the building and bring a little of God's creation indoors."

"A few nice pot plants would do that, and we could look at the flowers as we came in. As it is, Daphne cuts them Saturday night and they're mostly dead by Monday when I come in to clean up."

"Nonetheless, we will be having flowers. Daphne likes arranging them and I love to see them."

AND that was the end of it, although Albert continued to sigh deeply as Daphne arrived each Sunday with her buckets full of flowers. In spring and summer she trawled through the gardens of the congregation, whilst in winter she had to dip into the inadequate Flower Fund, with more meagre results.

Whatever the season, Daphne arranged, Albert sighed and Harriet kept the peace.

Albert was even more confused by Daphne's assertion that sticking a few flowers in a vase was "art". She'd done courses in flower arranging, even had a diploma, apparently.

Once, she'd tried explaining it all to him.

"Look at these." She'd waved her hand at a bowl of ferns and yellow flowers. "In the ground, these were just flowers. But when I arrange them I can make them anything I want — they become more than they were."

He tried to understand, he really did. He put his head on one side and tried to see how she'd made the flowers more than they really were, but all he could see was a bowl of

49

ferns and yellow flowers, which would have looked better in the garden.

Next Sunday was going to be Mothering Sunday, when all the children would come to chapel with their mums. Albert overheard Daphne telling Harriet that she was going to fill the chapel with daffodils for the service.

"Clouds of daffodils. The flowers round the chapel will be out next week, so I'm going to come on Saturday to cut them. That way, they'll have time to open up and be at their best for the service. And I'll make sure we have plenty for the children to take home."

Daphne's face was alight, and Harriet was smiling at her enthusiasm.

Albert was not smiling.

"You'd be better leaving them flowers where they are, and where God intended them to be."

Harriet gave him a "Haven't we been here before?" look, but Daphne was crestfallen.

"Oh, but Mr Downing, the chapel looks so beautiful when it's all decked out, and the children love having flowers to take home after the service. I won't cut them all. I'll leave some to be a show outside."

"I'm sure you will." Albert shook his head, then buttoned up his coat and set off to cross the street to his bungalow. He walked up the short drive, admiring his own display of spring bulbs. Another week, and his daffodils would be in full bloom.

THE following Saturday Albert woke up at seven, turned over and went back to sleep for another hour and a half. Without Grace, he didn't feel the need to be up and about so early.

By 9.30 a.m. he was in the kitchen, making tea and eating toast by the window. He rarely bothered sitting at the table these days.

He had a clear view of the chapel from his window and, as he waited for the kettle to boil, he thought something looked different — not quite right. He couldn't place what it was, though.

Albert sighed, wondering if he was due to have his eyes tested. Grace had always kept him up to date with things like dentists and opticians.

He made his tea, and spread a copy of the local paper in front of him. Ten minutes, then he'd do a bit in the garden. As he skimmed the stories of petty theft and amateur theatre productions he found his thoughts slipping away to Daphne, and wondering whether she had massacred the daffodils yet.

She only lived a five-minute walk away, in one of the old railway houses, with her widowed brother and his two teenage sons. She'd never married, apparently. Albert thought the boys were away at college or in the Army or something — not around, anyway.

Thwaite, North Yorkshire, England

*A*S soon as I saw the cover painting of Thwaite, I was taken back to the days when one of my pals and I used to stay in the town to explore the nearby Yorkshire Dales. Those handsome stone houses, so typical of Dales' architecture, made for a homely place to spend an evening by the fireside after a long walk on the moors above.

My pal and I had always lived and worked in the city of Hull, but we made a point of our annual trips up into the hills. Even though we were only able to do it once a year, we both agreed that there was no finer way to blow off the cobwebs than with a brisk walk around Swaledale on a lovely day such as the one in your painting.

Many thanks for the memories.

— *Mr A.C., Hull.*

J. CAMPBELL KERR.

He couldn't imagine Daphne coping with teenagers in the house, somehow, but from what he heard they thought the world of her.

"A surprising woman," he mused, as he took a final bite of toast and finished his tea. He knew she worked as a bookkeeper for a furniture company in the village, and again he couldn't quite see how fluttery Daphne coped with the demands of a busy business.

"Definitely a surprising woman."

He dumped his cup and plate in the sink, swept the toast crumbs after them and pulled his gardening jacket from the back of the chair, where it had been mouldering since a rather damp midweek outing.

HE was pottering in the front garden an hour or so later when Daphne arrived at the chapel, with a couple of wicker baskets slung on her arms and a silly, happy look on her face.

"Poor daffodils," he muttered and thought about going into the back garden. But the sun was warmer in the front and he was enjoying the song of a blackbird in the hawthorn hedge, so he stayed, cutting back the dead bits and tidying up the beds.

The shriek frightened off the blackbird and left Albert staring round in confusion and clutching his back, having jarred it from rising too quickly. Daphne came rushing across the road, secateurs in hand and a look of desolation on her face.

"Oh, Mr Downing, have you seen what they've done? My beautiful daffodils!"

She seemed about to cry, alarming Albert. He straightened up properly, stretching his back and looking at her.

"What who's done? And what about the daffodils?" She was more baffling than usual.

"They've taken all my daffodils. Look!" She waved a hand in the direction of the chapel and began to cry properly. It didn't suit her.

Albert looked, and saw what he had missed this morning. No wonder the chapel had looked different. Where, yesterday, there had been a swathe of gold, cheerful and pretty against the brick wall, now there was only a sad collection of leaves and broken stems.

Every single flower had been taken. It was a crying shame.

"Well, they're gone all right. It'll be kids, I reckon. I saw those Curtis boys hanging around again last night. You should have a word with their grandmother — she lets them run wild."

Albert shook his head and started to bend down again, one hand carefully supporting the small of his back.

"But what are we going to do now?"

Daphne had a surprisingly high-pitched voice when she was upset, Albert realised.

"Do now? Well, I'm going to finish this bit of gardening, and then I'll probably have some lunch." He picked up his trowel.

"But what about the chapel? How am I going to decorate it?"

Albert didn't like plaintive women. They made him uncomfortable. Grace had never been plaintive. Reluctantly, he eased himself up again and looked at Daphne.

"I don't know what you're going to do. I never understood why you wanted to fill the chapel with flowers in the first place. Besides, there's no need to get so upset. You were going to cut them all down anyway."

Daphne gave him a hurt look, which made him wonder if he'd been a bit harsh. Then she turned away.

"I would report it to the police, though. Can't have this sort of thing going unreported," he called after her.

She didn't reply, just wandered back towards the chapel, her secateurs trailing from her hand. Feeling strangely unsettled, Albert decided to call it a day and take an early lunch.

SUNDAY dawned, another bright day but with a chill in the air. Albert rose early, as ever hoping to be first to chapel. This morning he was beaten only by Harriet, who seemed to have caught her mood from the weather and was distinctly frosty, he thought.

Mrs Penny slipped into her place at the organ as Albert was setting out the notice sheets but there was no sign of Daphne. No sign of any flowers in the chapel, either. Funny how plain it looked by the pulpit, and over in the window recess.

Albert thought there was a real air of sadness over the whole chapel without the colour and brightness of the usual flowers.

Over half the congregation had arrived before Daphne appeared. She was pale, and muttered only a brief good morning before edging into her pew. Throughout the service Albert felt his eyes drawn to her. She looked so sad, with none of her usual sparkle. Funny what arranging flowers did to people.

He turned back to his hymn sheet. Mrs Penny was playing the opening bars of one of the newfangled songs the minister liked. He must be getting used to them, because this one didn't sound half as bad as he remembered. He even sang a couple of the choruses.

Harriet must have begged or stolen a few flowers from somewhere, because there were some limp carnations for the children to take home. Not the same as daffodils, somehow.

After the service there was usually tea and biscuits and a

Fair Trade stall. Daphne always helped, but today she drooped over the tea table, looking desperate to be away. Even the children didn't elicit a smile from her.

Albert finished tidying the hymn books and went to collect a coffee from Daphne. He was just stirring in his sugar when Jean Curtis bustled her way over to them.

"Daphne, you'll never guess what my boys have done today!"

Albert shot her a look. He could well guess.

"Your grandsons — Kyle and Michael?" Daphne sounded wary.

"Yes! I know they can be trouble, but they're good at heart. Imagine, this morning, when I came downstairs, they presented me with the biggest bunch of daffodils you've ever seen! For a special grandmother, they said."

JEAN CURTIS was glowing with pride. Albert thought it a shame he was going to have to bring her back to earth with a crash. He had opened his mouth to speak, but before he had a chance, Daphne cut right across him.

"Oh, Jean, that's lovely. What a thoughtful thing to do. They must have saved up all their pocket money."

Albert stared, quite speechless in his admiration of this surprising woman. Daphne met his gaze and held it for a long moment.

Then she looked away and Albert stuttered.

"Very kind of the lads, Jean. Very kind indeed." He coughed and turned away.

Later, after his solitary lunch, Albert went into the garden with a pair of kitchen scissors and carefully cut two dozen of his best daffodils. He wrapped them in a sheet of tissue-paper and walked round to Daphne's house. She answered the door straight away, looking a little flustered.

"Mr Downing, goodness, whatever are you doing here?"

"It's Albert. And I brought these for you. From the garden."

He thrust the flowers into her arms and was about to march off home when she called after him.

"Would you like to stay for tea? I've made orange cake."

Daphne peered over the top of her daffodils and Albert thought she was very pretty when she smiled.

He took off his cap.

"I'd be delighted."

The following year, Mothering Sunday was celebrated with the biggest display of flowers the congregation had ever known. Daphne and Albert Downing had grown enough daffodils in their own garden to fill the chapel . . . and still have a few over for the Curtis boys to give to their grandmother! ■

Getting To Know Sam

by Linda Mitchelmore.

Illustration by
John Hancock.

ALL the way over on the ferry, Rhona felt queasy. It wasn't supposed to be like this. The brochure featured people lazing about on loungers in the sunshine; sitting at a bar, a cocktail in their hands; happy families leaning on their arms against the rail, gazing out on to an azure sea.

Well, they were as far removed from a happy family as they could be at the moment — she and Brad, her husband, and her stepson, Sam, who was being moody, rude and tearful in turn.

"*Mal de mer*?" Brad said, as Rhona clasped a hand to her mouth. "French for seasick."

"I don't know," Rhona said. "I've never been on a ferry before. Of course, it could be . . ."

Brad stopped her, resting a hand on her shoulder and giving it an affectionate squeeze.

"Not yet," he whispered. He nodded towards the rail where Sam was throwing crisps to a seagull. "Sam's got too many firsts at the moment — first holiday without his mum, a new stepmum . . ."

But Sam must have heard because he wheeled round and stared hatefully at Rhona.

"My mummy was never seasick," he said.

"Yes, she was," Brad said.

That was the good thing about Brad — he knew his son was always trying to wind Rhona up and he always stepped in and stopped him. Rhona knew it was only natural that six-year-old Sam was missing his mum, Laura, because she'd been his main carer after her separation from Brad.

But her fatal car accident had changed everything. It was at her funeral, six months ago, that Rhona had met Sam for the first time, too.

Now here they were, with Roscoff at last appearing on the horizon, on their way to what Brad had cheerily — and in Rhona's opinion, over-optimistically — called a "bonding" holiday for Rhona and Sam.

"Do you want to drive?" he asked her.

They'd reached the hold and squeezed themselves between tightly parked cars to get to their own.

"You drive," Rhona said. "It's my first time in Brittany, remember? I'll sightsee."

She slipped into the passenger seat while Brad strapped Sam securely in the back. If she didn't turn round, Rhona wouldn't see his angry little stares in her direction, would she?

SAM was a beautiful child; tow-coloured hair, sturdy arms and legs that would be muscled like his father's as he grew. There had to be a way to get him to like her — if only she could find it.

They stopped at a small town for lunch. Rhona was enchanted. Narrow streets criss-crossed to the edge of a hill with a spectacular view down to the river. She could see the old bridge — crumbling now, but still beautiful — next to the new one. A bright red canoe sliced through the velvety ribbon of water and disappeared round a bend in the river.

"Picnic or restaurant?" Brad said.

"Picnic!" Sam punched the air.

Brad raised a questioning eyebrow at Rhona.

"A picnic's fine with me, too," she said.

He nodded.

"But first a drink, I think. Something cold. What would you like, Rhona?"

"Orange will be fine. What flavour is your juice, Sam?" Rhona asked, even though she knew very well what flavour it was.

"Don't know," Sam said with a pout.

"Yes, you do," Brad admonished.

"I don't any more," Sam said. He tucked his hands under his armpits and turned his back on Brad and Rhona.

Brad shrugged and mouthed "Sorry" at Rhona. He reached for her hand and held it firmly, massaging her thumb with his own.

"It's OK," she whispered. "Give it time."

Rhona relaxed a little going from *boulangerie* to *charcuterie* to *alimentation générale* buying the components of their picnic, although how Brad thought they were going to eat the mountain of things he'd bought she didn't know. She was still feeling a bit queasy.

"Cakes," Sam said. "We haven't got any cakes."

"There's a *pâtisserie* over there," Rhona said. "Come and help me choose something, Sam."

"I don't want one now," he said.

"Well, we're buying some. Wait there, Rhona, we won't be long." Brad marched his son across the road.

Brad was, she knew, more than likely giving Sam a talking-to about his attitude because they were a long time choosing what amounted to three cakes exquisitely packed in a box and tied with ribbon. They strolled down a narrow lane to the river to eat their picnic. But it was a strained time for them all. Even swans gliding by and Canada geese pestering for breadcrumbs did nothing to cheer up Sam.

What on earth it was going to be like when they got to Les Hirondelles, Rhona didn't even want to imagine. Les Hirondelles had been where Sam had spent every single holiday of his young life — most of them with both his parents, until the separation. It would be like coming home for him, which was why Brad had decided to rent the same *gîte*.

It had seemed like a good idea when Brad had mooted the plan, but now Rhona wasn't so sure.

"OH, it's wonderful, Brad," Rhona said.

Brad turned the car off the road and on to a narrow, cobbled track. At the end of the track Rhona could see a long house made of the local stone, with blue shutters closed to keep out the sun. On the right was a meadow, the grass studded with yellow daisies. Apple trees, in fresh green leaf, were studded randomly through it. It would be teeming with wildlife — Rhona couldn't wait to explore. She'd brought cameras and her painting things — this was going to be perfect.

"The grass needs cutting," Brad said. "Part of the reason I get this place so cheaply is because I mow the meadow when I arrive, and again when I leave."

"No, don't mow it," Rhona said. "Not yet, anyway. Please."

"Sam loves going on the ride-on mower," Brad said. He pulled the car to a stop and looked over to the back seat. Sam was still asleep.

"Could you leave it for a few days?"

"OK," Brad agreed with a smile.

IT was three days before Rhona got a chance to go into the meadow. Sam had wanted to go to the beach, so that was what they did two days in a row.

The sand at Benodet was white and soft and the whole beach mercifully empty. Rhona enjoyed it more than she'd imagined she would. They'd paddled, all three of them, even though the sea was icily

Garden Glories!

THERE'S something almost bridal about the Camellia Bushfield. The beautiful cream and yellow flowers look as if they should have pride of place in a bridal bouquet, and the glossy green leaves only serve to emphasis their fresh, bright appearance.

This is a hardy camellia and, believe it or not, these exotic flowers can reach up to 10cm across in size! They have a spreading effect and are ideal against a sheltered wall. Eventually your camellia will reach a height of 1.8-2m. A real beauty, this is one to enjoy looking at all summer long!

cold. They ate lunch outside on a café terrace — langoustines and *pommes frites*, and the yummiest chocolate mousse Rhona had ever eaten.

Then Sam had wanted ice-cream and stamped his feet and cried until Brad gave in.

"I'll make it up to you, darling," he told Rhona that night as they got into bed, both of them exhausted coping with Sam and his tantrums.

"I know. It's just that it's so hard. Sam kicks against me all the time. If I try to hold his hand he pulls away."

"Oh, darling," Brad said, kissing the top of Rhona's head. "I've got an idea. You can say no if you don't like it."

Rhona nodded, intrigued.

"You've never been alone with Sam before, have you?"

She shook her head.

"Well, no. Not for more than a few minutes, and even then he wouldn't speak to me. He kept turning his back, or stomping off, or . . ."

Rhona felt tears welling. She shouldn't be letting a six-year-old upset her so much. She took a deep breath, then reached for a tissue on the bedside table.

"What's your idea?" she asked.

"I might need to take the car to the garage tomorrow. A bit of an oil leak, nothing much, but it'll need checking. There's no point in all of us going. I thought . . ."

Rhona touched a finger to his lips and laughed.

"I think I'm getting the picture! You think it would be a good idea if Sam and I stayed here and did something together?"

"Something like that," Brad said. He yawned. "It's just that I'm turning into a monster for him now when I have to keep telling him off when he's rude to you."

Rhona thought Brad looked so unutterably sad in that moment and her heart almost broke for him.

She leaned over and kissed Brad's cheek.

"OK," she said. "I'll stay with Sam, although I don't know what I'm going to say to him, or what we'll do."

"Don't worry about it now. Get some sleep, sweetheart. Who knows what tomorrow will bring?"

Tomorrow would be better, wouldn't it? It had to be.

In the morning Brad came into the kitchen as Rhona was making coffee. He said in a loud voice, so Sam could hear, that he'd noticed a problem with the car.

"Boring!" Sam said. He broke a croissant into pieces and began spreading each piece very messily with blackcurrant jam.

Rhona started to laugh, but Sam fixed her with the resentful stare he seemed to reserve just for her.

"I'll take it into the garage at Baud," Brad said. "It's quite close. The car will limp that far. No point in us all going." He leaned over to kiss Rhona.

"Yuk," Sam said, looking away. "Can I have cocoa?"

"Rhona will make it for you. OK?" Brad said.

"No!" Sam said. "My mummy made the best cocoa ever."

"She did," Brad agreed. "But Rhona's cocoa is pretty good, too, Sam. Give it a try? I won't be long, and when I get back you can tell me all about it."

He crossed his fingers for luck and smiled at Rhona and was gone.

BRAD seemed to have been gone a long time. Rhona had washed up the breakfast things, and made the beds. Sam had been told to go and wash, but she wasn't sure that her stepson had actually got wet, as there was still a smear of dried cocoa on his cheek. Rhona fought against the urge to find a flannel to wipe it off, because it was evidence that Sam had drunk the cocoa she'd made for him, even though he'd sat looking at it for a long time before he did.

Rhona had suggested doing a jigsaw, or that she could read Sam a story, but he didn't want to do either of those things.

"When's Daddy coming back?" Sam said. He folded his arms across his chest and gripped his shoulders.

"Soon," Rhona said.

"He will come back, won't he?"

"Of course," Rhona said, realising that Sam was worrying that Brad would suffer the same fate as Laura, and he'd be truly abandoned. Poor Sam.

"Well, when he comes back I'm going to tell him I want to go home. I hate it here now because my mummy's not here." Sam's bottom lip quivered.

"Oh, Sam," Rhona said. She knew she'd made a mistake staying indoors with all Laura's things around them. It was obvious Sam was having trouble with it all. "I know. We'll go outside, shall we?"

"I don't want to. I want my mummy. My real mummy. Not you."

Rhona crouched down next to Sam.

"Your real mummy loved you very, very, much and she will always be in your memory, but she can't come back."

That was what Brad and Rhona had agreed to say if Sam should ever talk about this.

"That's what Daddy said," Sam said, and Rhona thought she saw the beginnings of a smile — as though Sam was pleased Brad and Rhona were telling him the same story.

"And now I'm here to give you some love, too. There are all sorts of love, Sam."

Sam stuck his fist in his mouth and chewed on his knuckles. He didn't speak for ages.

"I love Connor," he said after a moment. "He's my best friend in all the world. He lets me play with his Nintendo. And I love his mummy, too, because she makes me chocolate brownies."

RHONA gulped back tears — Sam was beginning to understand more than he should at such a tender age. Sam had spent a lot of time at Connor's house after Laura had died — it was somewhere he knew, and Connor's mum had been so kind and understanding.

"I could make you chocolate brownies," Rhona said. "In fact, we could make them together."

Rhona knew that Laura had never done anything like that with Sam because cooking had been way down on her list of priorities. Rhona hadn't had to cook before she met Brad, but now that she did, she was loving it.

"I could eat some of the chocolate before it goes in the brownies," Sam said. "Connor's mummy lets me do that."

He looked up and his eyes met Rhona's and held her gaze for just a few seconds. Rhona felt her heart lift — Sam holding her gaze without a hateful stare was a breakthrough.

"Well, then, you can certainly eat some chocolate if you're doing the cooking!" Rhona said.

"Can we make them now?" Sam asked.

"Not just yet, but when Daddy comes back with the car, we will go to the shops and get the right ingredients. What do you think?" she asked him.

"I think that would be cool," Sam said, and punched the air. "But . . ." Sam went on, then hunched over, his head almost on the table.

"But what?" Rhona said.

"You might forget. Sometimes Mummy forgot . . ."

"I won't forget," Rhona said, stopping him. "I promise. Now then, I really need to go outside and I can't leave you here. But I've found this in the barn."

She held up a butterfly net on a long stick.

"What is it?"

"A butterfly net. You can carry it if you want to."

RHONA placed the butterfly net on the table and picked up her camera and her butterfly book, even though she knew most of the names of the more common sorts. She felt she'd started on a journey with Sam and now she couldn't turn back.

"Where are we going?" Sam asked. He reached out a hand and curled his fingers around the stick and slid the butterfly net towards him. He stared down at the table as he spoke.

"To the meadow."

"We can't. Daddy's got to mow it."

"Not yet, he hasn't," Rhona said. "I've got work to do in the meadow before Daddy mows it."

"What work?" Sam said.

"I've got to take photographs."

"Why?"

"It's what I do, remember? I take photographs and afterwards I paint the same picture. You've been in my studio at home, haven't you?"

"Not much," Sam said.

Only because you won't, Rhona thought with a sad sigh.

"Well, you can come any time you want to," she said, knowing that she sounded falsely bright and anxious.

"Have you got chocolate brownies in your studio?" Sam said. Again he looked up at Rhona and held her gaze, but he pressed his lips together as though he was trying not to smile, trying not to let Rhona know he was beginning to like her just a little bit, even if it was the promise of chocolate brownies that was swaying his opinion.

"Yes," Rhona said with a broad smile. She made a mental note always to have brownies in her studio in case Sam decided to cross the threshold.

"Now, shall we go and see what we can find to photograph in the meadow?"

Sam slid down off the chair, dragging the butterfly net with him.

"All right," he said.

THEY crossed the road and Rhona lifted the latch on the gate to enter the meadow.

"What are you going to take photographs of?" Sam asked.

"Butterflies. Now, step very carefully and slowly and tell me if you see a butterfly."

"Yes!" Sam said. "There's one. It's blue. Like a piece of sky has fallen down. Oh, no, it's flying away again, back to the sky."

"I've never thought of it like that," Rhona said. "But we have to be quiet, too. Talk in whispers." Rhona put a finger to her lips. "Sssh. Look, it's coming back again."

"What's it called?" Sam whispered.

"The Common Blue. It's got another name as well — *Polyommatus icarus.* That's its scientific name."

Sam seemed satisfied with her answer and was mercifully quiet as Rhona took photos of the Common Blue.

"Shall we look for another butterfly now?" Sam looked at Rhona, a half-smile on his face, as though he badly wanted to help her but didn't know how.

Rhona returned his smile. Was she beginning to get through to Sam at last? And more important, was he beginning to accept her and all she would be in his life from now on?

They were both on a steep learning curve and it was as though they both knew it.

"Good idea," Rhona said. "Look! I think I can see something else over there. If we sit quietly and watch, you'll see all the patterns on its wings."

"The grass is too long," Sam said.

"It has to be long for the butterflies," Rhona said.

She held out her hand towards Sam, but he didn't take it.

"How do butterflies get in your tummy, Rhona?" Sam asked instead.

Rhona held out her hand towards Sam again and this time he slipped his hand into hers. Rhona clasped her fingers more firmly around Sam's small, warm hand but he whisked it away again. Too soon, Rhona chided herself, too soon.

"Tell me how butterflies get in your tummy," Sam said.

"They don't. It's just a feeling. See that yellow butterfly over there flapping its wings?"

Sam nodded.

"Well, that flapping is like the feeling you get in your tummy when you're worried about things."

"Sort of fluttery."

Bus Pass

THEY gave to me a bus pass
And said "Go where you like,
We know the days have come and gone
When you could ride your bike.

"Your carbon footprint's shrinking
When you leave the car at home,
So come with us, get on a bus
And let us help you roam."

But I've been here for ages,
And a bus I haven't seen,
I'm feeling cold and turning blue
Instead of going green!

I had an urge to wander
And to venture far and wide,
I'd packed myself a lunch
That I could peck at on the ride.

Now I'm not one to get upset,
Nor one to make a fuss,
But it's no use to have a pass
If you don't have a bus!

I'll wait a little longer,
After all, I've come this far,
But if it doesn't come by twelve,
I'm off to fetch the car!

— Pam Davies.

Willie Shand.

"That's it exactly."

"I get that a lot," Sam said.

"Do you?" Rhona said. Her heart went out to him. "When?"

"When I go to nursery and birthday parties and I remember Mummy can't fetch me any more.

"And when I have to do new things," Sam went on. "My tummy goes all wobbly."

"We all feel like that about new things."

"Do you, Rhona?"

Rhona nodded. She had a fluttery, butterfly feeling in her tummy right now, and it had nothing to do with being anxious. One wrong word and she could put distance between her and Sam, just as they were beginning to get to know one another.

"What's the yellow one called?" Sam asked suddenly, his attention taken by the butterfly.

"That's a Clouded Yellow. Or *Colias croceus*."

"Will I have to have another name like the butterflies now you're my new mummy?"

"Is that giving you butterflies in your tummy?"

"Yes. So will I have to have another name?"

"No, you'll always be Sam."

Poor Sam. So many things his young mind didn't understand. And sitting here in the sunshine, with only the sounds of the birds and bees and the breeze in the willows down by the stream, Rhona would help him understand.

Rhona told him that his daddy loved him very much and that by Christmas he was going to have a baby brother or sister.

BABIES cry," Sam said. "Connor's baby sister screams and screams."

"All babies scream sometimes," Rhona said. "But babies go back to sleep if you give them some milk to drink."

Sam looked serious for a moment.

"I don't think Connor's mummy knows about the milk. I'll tell her when we go home."

Rhona had to clap a hand to her mouth so that she didn't laugh, because Sam was quite serious.

"I don't want a baby sister. Can you give it back if it's a baby sister?"

"No, Sam. We'll love it if it's a boy or a girl. Just like your daddy and mummy loved you when you were born."

"Did I scream and scream?"

"Oh, I expect so," Rhona said. "Mummies and daddies love their babies even when they scream."

Sam screwed up his forehead, deep in concentration.

"I could give it some milk if it screams," he said.

"That will be good," Rhona said. "That's just what big brothers do."

She was rewarded with a grin — the first real grin she'd seen Sam give her in the time she'd known him.

SHE hoped Brad wouldn't be cross that she was having this conversation on her own with Sam about the baby, because they'd agreed they would do it together. But somehow, now seemed exactly the right time to tell Sam.

"And there's another reason why we get butterflies in our tummy," Rhona said. "Well, why ladies do. It's when the baby starts to move inside my tummy, stretching its little arms and legs. The baby did it just now for the first time."

Sam touched his tummy, looking puzzled.

"Does Daddy know about the baby moving?"

"Not yet," Rhona said, glad now that she'd been with Sam when she'd first felt the baby move.

"It can be our secret," Sam said, looking serious. "I won't tell."

"Just for a little while, then." Rhona laughed.

"Will the baby have two names like the butterflies? I've got two names. I'm Samuel Noah, but everyone calls me Sam."

"Well, you could choose one name and Daddy and I will choose the other. How would that be?"

"Can I?" Sam clapped his hands together in excitement, making a shower of butterflies take flight. He watched them fly away.

"I don't think my real mummy knew about butterflies . . ." His voice trailed away.

"Not everybody does, Sam. I expect there were lots of things your mummy knew that I don't."

"My real mummy sings better than you."

Sam had used the present tense as though Laura was still alive — and for Sam, Rhona knew, she still was in his mind and his heart.

"Everyone sings better than I do." Rhona laughed. "I sing like a frog with a sore throat."

"I like frogs. Frogs are funny," Sam said.

He patted the back of Rhona's hand. Was he trying to tell her he thought she said funny things and he liked that, but didn't quite know how to put it into words? Rhona hoped so.

And then, into the silence of the meadow came the distinctive sound of Brad's car.

"Daddy's back," Rhona said.

"Shall we go and tell him about the baby?" Sam gripped the butterfly net with one hand, and slipped his other one into Rhona's. And this time he didn't pull away again.

Hand in hand, Rhona and Sam walked through the yellow daisies to meet Brad — how wonderful it felt. ■

W HAT'S the matter, darling?" Kate asked as Lauren entered the back door and slumped down at the kitchen table.

"It's nothing." Lauren sighed, leaning on her elbows.

"I may not be the world's most intuitive person, but I do know when something is troubling my own daughter." Kate pulled off her rubber gloves and sat down opposite Lauren. "Come on. Out with it."

"It's just that Melissa's dad is hiring a vintage Buick to take her and her cousins to the prom and Amanda's dad is taking her in an articulated lorry."

"Oh, I see."

It was at times like this that Kate wished Lauren's father, Rory, was still there, fulfilling a rôle which, sometimes, only a dad could fill in spite of a mother's best efforts to be both parents.

Instead, Rory had abdicated all parental responsibility and walked out when Lauren was a toddler after deciding he no longer wanted to feel trapped.

Kate had had no idea she had ever made Rory feel trapped. She was the one who had sacrificed her own career aspirations. In fact, she felt that Rory had enjoyed far more freedom than many of her friends' husbands.

Still, it was water under the bridge now. Kate had done her grieving many years ago — Rory was not coming back and had decided against having any form of contact with them — and she had poured her energy into raising Lauren, the beautiful sixteen-year-old daughter who was sitting opposite her now, resting her head in her cupped hands, wishing for a father who would never have any inkling of the importance of this occasion.

T HE school leavers' prom had actually become quite an occasion in the town with the girls dressing up in beautiful ball-gowns, the boys sporting tuxedos and everyone arriving at the venue — an upmarket hotel overlooking the sea — in lavish or unusual modes of transport. Photographs of the event were even spread across several pages of the local newspaper.

"What about Kirstie and Hannah or your other friends?"

Illustration by
Shane Marsh.

Hopefully

by Gwen Rollinson.

"They're hiring a stretch limo."

"Couldn't you go with them?"

"It would still be too expensive." Lauren shrugged her shoulders in resignation.

"I'm so sorry, love. I wish I could afford . . ."

"It's all right, Mum. I'm not blaming you. You've already paid for the ticket and the fabric to make me a dress."

Kate reached across and took her daughter's hand.

"You deserve it, love."

Lauren had never complained about their lack of money and had even taken a Saturday job to help out. Now that her exams were over, Lauren was also looking for extra work to save enough to supplement the small grant she would receive when she attended college to train in animal care the following September.

Fortunately, Kate had managed to save a small amount from her administrator's wages each month to buy the prom ticket and some pretty,

67

shiny fabric.

If she couldn't afford to hire a limo, at least she would ensure her daughter had a stunning gown to wear, and Kate knew she would be lining up along the street with the other proud mums taking photographs on the night.

"We could always decorate Suzie." Kate's eyes lit up as she thought of the clapped-out, navy blue Fiesta festooned with garlands and ribbons. After all, the trend was for students to arrive in unusual as well as lavish modes of transport.

"It's OK, Mum." Lauren giggled. "I don't mind going in Suzie as she is, but could we park round the corner?"

"Cheeky madam." Kate squeezed Lauren's hand again. Where was the fairy godmother with a pumpkin when you needed her? "At least you're laughing. Now, how about I make scrambled eggs on toast for lunch and then we can have another fitting of the dress?"

"Tell you what. Why don't I do the eggs?" Lauren stood up and walked over to the sink to wash her hands.

"That sounds good to me. There's a new tray of eggs in the fridge. Pete the farmer dropped them in earlier." Kate suddenly smiled to herself. They only knew one Pete, but for some reason they always called him "Pete the farmer".

"I like Pete. He's nice," Lauren said. She caught her mother's eye. "He's single, too . . ."

"All right, Miss Matchmaker, I agree — he is a nice man."

PETE had taken over the running of Hill Top Farm after his dad had suffered a bout of pneumonia a couple of years ago, and Kate had got to know him when she had started walking to the farm to buy fresh eggs from his mother. Lately, he had taken to bringing the eggs round in person.

"Did you invite him in for a coffee?" Lauren's eyebrows raised in hope. Kate shook her head sheepishly.

"I thought he might have things to do."

"He came round in person to bring you eggs and you thought he might have other things to do?" Lauren tutted at her mother.

Kate bit her lip.

"I'll invite him in next time."

Lauren rolled her eyes.

"I will," Kate insisted.

For a moment she felt as thought their rôles had been reversed and that she was suddenly the sixteen-year-old daughter.

As with other areas of her life, Kate had put any thoughts of romance on hold, too, but she had always reasoned that she was too busy raising a child single-handedly to have time to nurture any new relationship.

Now she recognised it for the excuse it was — a way of avoiding having to meet, let alone trust, another man ever again . . .

"This is gorgeous," Lauren said, sashaying around the lounge in the floor-length dress a week later.

"Careful," Kate warned, "it's still only tacked in parts." She kneeled down to adjust the length of the hem and pinned it in place.

The silvery-blue satin fabric had been the perfect choice, Kate thought as she stood back to admire the dress falling in soft folds against Lauren's slim figure, accentuated by the gentle ruching just above her hips.

"You should have been a fashion designer, Mum. You're really talented. You should do it for a living."

"I did think about it once, but it never seemed the right time to start." Kate recalled her days at college when she had won several awards for her designs, but she had put any thoughts of a career on hold when she married Rory. Soon after the wedding, Kate had discovered she was pregnant. It wasn't an easy pregnancy, and Kate had had sickness for many months, which dampened any thoughts of a career.

When Lauren was born, she had even less time to follow her dream and, after Rory left and Lauren started nursery school, it was more important to find a job that paid a regular wage rather than concentrate on starting a risky dress-making business.

Fortunately, however, Kate had still managed to put her skills to good use, enabling her to clothe both Lauren and herself at very little cost. She would buy clothes from the local charity shops and alter them to her own designs — often to the envy of her friends.

Her creations were also admired by the mothers Kate chatted to at the school gates whilst waiting to collect Lauren and it wasn't long before she had several requests to make outfits for them, too.

Not only did it keep her occupied during the evenings after Lauren was in bed, but it also meant that, to some extent, she was fulfilling her dreams. It helped pay a few bills, too!

PERHAPS now *is* the right time to start." Lauren gave her mother a hug. Kate had certainly had a steady flow of orders. In fact, recently and regretfully she had had to turn down a request to make bridesmaids' dresses because she had already agreed to make costumes for a local dance troupe and, more importantly, she wanted time to make her own daughter's prom dress.

Perhaps now, however, was the time to consider reducing her hours as an administrator to concentrate more on dress-making.

"Whatever did I do to deserve such a wonderful daughter?" Kate hugged her back. "And when did you grow to be so wise?"

Kate continued to work on the dress that afternoon while Lauren took a couple of carrots to feed Rosie and Jess, Pete's donkeys. Their field was only a ten-minute walk from home and Lauren regularly took them carrots or apples, having fallen in love with the gentle animals the first time she set eyes on them.

Kate often suspected it was Rosie and Jess who first kindled Lauren's interest in animal care as a career.

During the following week, Kate kept mulling over the possibility of developing her dress-making into a proper business. She was still young enough to pursue her dream, and if she didn't do it now, then when would she do it?

Kate knew she didn't want to look back years from now and regret not having tried. A spark had been re-ignited which she didn't want to quell again.

✳   ✳   ✳   ✳

The following weekend, Kate finished Lauren's dress and spent the afternoon jotting down ideas and designs at the kitchen table whilst Lauren was at her Saturday job at the newsagent's.

Garden Glories!

WE all have walls or fences in our gardens that just look too bare. If you've been thinking about a climbing plant, you might want to take a look at Campsis "Indian Summer". The apricot-coloured flowers are most unusual and there is a spectacular abundance of them.

Not as tall as other campsis, it would also make an attractive pot plant if you only have a balcony or small patio. A rapid climber, this campsis would be an asset to any boring wall or fence. One word of warning, though — in colder districts this climber does need the protection of a warm south-facing wall.

She could put an advertisement in the local paper — perhaps they could even do a feature on her with a few photographs of her designs . . .

A knock at the door brought her back to the present.

"Fresh eggs." Pete smiled, stepping into the kitchen and setting the tray down on the worktop.

"Thanks, Pete."

"You've been busy." Pete indicated the pieces of paper, filled with sketches and scribbles, strewn across the table.

"Yes, I am busy," Kate responded without thinking.

"Oh . . . I'd best leave you to it then." A forlorn expression replaced the cheerful smile and Kate realised how ungrateful she must have sounded, which hadn't been her intention at all. She was just wrapped up in a chain of thoughts.

"Sorry, Pete, I didn't mean . . ." She took a deep breath. "Would you like a coffee?"

"I'd love one." The smile returned to Pete's face — a smile which, Kate noticed, extended to the crinkles at the corners of his pale blue eyes. She had

70

never actually noticed how handsome he was — or more probably had tried to ignore it — until now, and when he flicked his blond tousled hair away from his face, she noticed his muscular forearms were tanned from working outdoors.

A slight tingle ran down her spine — a sensation she had not felt in a very long time — and she could hear Lauren's encouraging voice inside her head saying, "Go for it, Mum."

AS they drank their coffee, Kate told Pete about her tentative plans to develop a dress design business. She found Pete to be a very good listener and with his encouraging comments and ideas Kate suddenly felt she could actually make her dream a reality.

She would do it properly, of course, no rushing into it in a foolhardy manner. She wasn't about to give up her day job entirely, at least not until she knew she could make a reasonable living from her new venture.

She had also noticed that the local college ran short courses on setting up a business so she would enrol on the next one — after all, dress-making was one thing, but running a business was an entirely different matter and if she was going to do it at all she would make sure she did it armed with as much knowledge as possible.

"Whenever you're ready I'd be happy to help you set up a website," Pete said. "It's actually a hobby of mine."

They talked their way through a second mug of coffee as comfortably as if they had known each other for years. Kate confided in Pete about Lauren's transport dilemma and laughed with him as she recounted her ideas for decorating Suzie.

"Maybe that's something else I could help you with," Pete said after they had regained composure. "I've just had an idea . . ."

He shifted awkwardly in his chair.

"I'll help you on the condition that you have dinner with me."

"Agreed," Kate said without hesitation.

It was a condition that she would be very happy to accept. She had reached

71

the stage in her life where it was time finally to cast away her former doubts and insecurities and begin to trust again.

❋   ❋   ❋   ❋

"Lauren, it's quarter to seven, " Kate called up the stairs.

Lauren had spent several hours getting ready and Kate didn't want her to be late for her grand arrival at the Gainsborough Hotel, the venue for the prom.

Lauren appeared at the top of the stairs, radiant in her elegant gown. Kate thought it didn't seem two minutes since Lauren was starting nursery school and now here she was, a young woman, ready to take on the world.

"You look beautiful, darling." Kate wiped a tear from her eye as she aimed her camera lens at Lauren.

"You'll start me off in a minute, Mum," Lauren protested.

"There'll be no tears on that dress, missy," Kate said firmly. "Now we really should leave."

OUTSIDE, Lauren headed towards the Fiesta
"We're not taking Suzie." Kate smiled enigmatically. "Pete's taking us down."

"Pete?" Lauren gazed at her mother.

"I invited him in for that coffee . . ." Kate found it impossible to suppress a rather large smile. "While you're at the prom, he's taking me out to dinner."

"Good for you, Mum. I told you he was a nice man." Lauren winked.

The sound of clip clopping interrupted their conversation.

"That sounds like Pete," Kate said, laughing as she observed her daughter's puzzled expression.

"Your carriage awaits!" Kate motioned to Lauren as a cart, decorated with flowers and ribbons and pulled by two donkeys, drew up outside the house.

"Rosie and Jess!" Lauren shouted in delight.

Pete jumped down from his seat.

"You both look stunning." He smiled at Kate and Lauren. "I hope the transport meets with your approval."

"It's just perfect," Lauren said as she stepped forward to stroke the donkeys' heads. Pete helped Kate up on to the bench seat and turned to help Lauren.

"Your mum's responsible for the decoration," Pete informed her.

"Oh, Pete, this is great!" Lauren ran up to him and planted a kiss on his cheek.

"You're very welcome. We couldn't have you arriving for your big night in anything else." He helped her to sit down on the seat behind and took his place beside Kate.

As they set off slowly down the road, Kate still had a huge smile on her face.

The prom didn't just celebrate the end of an era for Lauren, it signified the start of a new chapter in her daughter's life, and with Pete beside her as well as her plans for a new business venture, Kate felt it signified the same for her, too . . . ■

None But The Brave...

by Linda Chloe Elmon.

I DRAGGED the dusty old leather Gladstone bag from the bottom of the cupboard.

"You should find plenty of stuff here for your history project, Amy."

Lots of young people nowadays are interested in their roots, and my great-granddaughter Amy had been after me, as family ancient, to tell her about the generations of proud men and women who'd served their country.

"Look at all this, Gran-gran. It's brilliant!"

The little ones had always called me "Gran-gran" to distinguish me from their non-great gran, Beth, my daughter; a habit they carried on even as teenagers.

Illustration by David Young.

The old bag was crammed with certificates, letters, paybooks, forms, documents and so on. Us Faulkners have always been in uniform: soldiers, sailors, aircrew, policemen, firemen, WRENS, wartime clippies and nurses. And the Forces like generating paperwork!

There was even a large, discoloured pawn ticket, but not too many old photographs.

In the days before WWI, it was a major event getting your picture taken.

"Everyone looks so fierce," Amy said, holding a couple of sepia studio portraits showing earnest young people in rough khaki, or sombre-looking fathers in tight collars and bowlers, and mothers in gowns and lace in front of a set-up background of a pillar with a potted plant.

These were my great-grandparents, grandparents, uncles, aunts . . . my family.

I think Amy was a bit disappointed at finding so many documents but only a few stiff, formal photos.

"But what were they like, Gran-gran?"

That was a difficult question, and was the reason why the next Saturday found Amy and me at the other end of the country visiting the place where not only my mum and dad had come from, but at least four generations of our lot.

George and I would have lived there, too, if his job hadn't dragged us to London soon after we married. My mum came with us because six weeks after we'd wed, my father died with his best friend in a car accident.

"It looks so historic, Gran-gran, with those cobblestones and half-wood houses."

Little had changed in that corner of the world and I'd hoped the place might give her a feel for her roots. We rode in a double-decker from the station.

"Do you know, this bus route is the one your great-aunt Daisy was clippie on for most of the war? That was before your mum was born. She had to wear a dark blue uniform. It was made of really uncomfortable hairy serge. I don't think you get it any more; at least, I haven't seen it for years. Daisy hated it. But a bomb stopped that."

Amy's mouth dropped open.

"A bomb? How?"

I HAD to smile at the memory, although at the time it wasn't a laughing matter.

"Well, a couple of German planes must've got lost because they just dumped their bombs before skedaddling home. It wasn't a proper raid or everyone would have been in the shelters. The impact blew my sister Daisy right off the bus."

Amy's eyes widened and her jaw dropped further.

"In those days the back of the bus was open," I explained.

"Oh, yes, I've seen those old buses in films. People could just jump on and off."

"Right, although Daisy didn't exactly jump. She went one way and most of her uniform went the other. Ticket machine, tickets, leather bag, sixpences, the lot."

"Oh, no, was she badly hurt?"

I could see the faint frown on Amy's face because as far as she knew, her great-aunt Daisy was hale and hearty at eighty-six this year.

"She had some scratches and bruises, and very few clothes left. But she

74

was mostly angry because she'd lost all her fares and tickets. She was interviewed by a chap from the radio and said being blown up was a lot less painful than having to wear that blessed serge uniform every day."

"She didn't!" Amy was delighted.

"Best thing was, a big clothing manufacturer was listening to the radio, and all the clippies got nice new uniforms as a result. As you can imagine, Daisy was very popular."

Amy gave a huge grin.

And it went on from there. Instead of showing her around the city sights as I'd planned, I showed her the places where her forebears had grown up and lived their lives.

"All these expensive flats along the canal were warehouses. Imagine it when it was a working dock, Amy, with ships tied up all the way along on both sides, hundreds of loaders, unloaders, clerks and so on. Then imagine everything ablaze.

"That's when my grandad and all the city's fire engines came to try to save the docks. It was just getting dark but all the reports said the fire was so fierce it was like daylight along the quayside.

"They were all given medals because, as you can see, the place is still standing."

We saw the early Victorian hospital, where I'd done some of my training before I joined the QARANC — Queen Alexandra's Royal Army Nursing Corps — and I showed her the dark alleys where my dad's brother walked the beat with a fellow constable.

"It's spooky, even now," Amy said in a low voice.

I nodded.

"In those days it was only safe for them to patrol in pairs, but a doctor carrying his bag could come and go without any trouble because they knew he was helping them."

We went to the light engineering industrial units that inhabited what used to be Blenheim Barracks.

"My dad, your great-great-grandad, brought me here as a child. He used to be in this room. He was a corporal then and shared with his best man, Mr Musgrove. We'll see his shop later."

"Two of them? But it's just a tiny storeroom," Amy said, looking around in amazement at the smallness of the area.

"Well, it is now, but they thought it was luxury. It was lovely then, Amy. Everything was painted white. Lanterns sparkling all along the verandas, polished brass. I thought it looked like a palace when I was little."

I could see Amy's imagination working overtime as she looked around the old parade square.

Victoria Avenue had been my favourite road as a youngster. On both sides were what people call "junk" shops. But to me they were Aladdin's caves, treasure stores filled with incredible relics and glimpses of the past.

There, I thought, we were bound to find some old postcards for Amy, showing the city's busy streets from the last century.

Musgrove's didn't seem one jot different. It was full of heavy, dark furniture, record players with silver horns, dusty books; cabinets full of lockets, rings, chains and watches; red uniform jackets and period dresses; gold-framed oil-paintings of landscapes or serious-faced officials; carved boxes; minor forests of canes and umbrellas; all crammed together in disorder.

In fact, it didn't look as if they'd shifted a single item in seventy years! I thought I even recognised a familiar antique or two as we worked our way slowly along, Amy fingering everything.

Then, with a jolt, I really did recognise something I never expected to see again — a polished, glass-topped mahogany case with purple velvet lining holding rows of shining belt buckles, mounted medals, ribbons and clasps.

Mum and Dad's "treasure chest" — tangible evidence of our family's service to the nation down the years.

"What's up, Gran-gran?"

"It's . . ." I could only point. I had lived with that case all my growing-up years, and the contents were imprinted in my memory. It had been stolen long, long ago, the month before George and I were married. I dropped helplessly into an ancient leather armchair.

"I'll get the assistant, Gran-gran. Don't faint!"

Amy rushed back to the counter at the front of the shop before I could tell her nothing was wrong.

Bellis Perennis

WHEN I'm tending my garden, I'm covered with guilt,
My bluebells have blight and my wallflowers wilt,
My apples have aphids, my roses have rot,
There's hardly one problem my garden's not got.
Just one thing alone gives me reason for pride,
A wonderful species you couldn't deride:
My Bellis Perennis are doing just fine,
My Bellis Perennis — how sweetly they shine,
When all else has perished, or shrivelled and curled,
Bright Bellis Perennis will conquer the world!
— Maggie Ingall.

THE memories came flooding back of Mr Musgrove, busily polishing with his thick, red duster. He was a lovely old man and I'd known him well. He had been in the car with Dad. They'd served together all their adult life in the Army. It was fitting they were together at the end. Mr Musgrove had known me from a little girl because I was always haunting the shop.

He had endless patience and knowledge, and I'd sometimes be there for hours among the rings, lockets, jewellery and beautiful silver boxes.

76

"You must pick out something for when you get married, Sally. I'll make it a wedding present for you."

But, of course, I never did. Even at fourteen I thought marriage a long way off.

Amy came back pulling a middle-aged chap who had the Musgrove high forehead and dimpled chin. He looked concerned.

"I'm all right," I said, pointing to the treasure chest, "but *they're* stolen goods."

"I don't think so. I recall they were there when I was at school," he said, obviously relieved that he didn't have a medical emergency to deal with.

"I don't mean recently," I snapped. "They were stolen before I got married. I remember I wrote out a description of the case and its contents to the police, for my dad."

He looked at me. Well, it was pretty clear I hadn't got married in the last decade or so, and I could see disbelief on his face.

"I'm talking about before you were born," I explained patiently. "This case is a family heirloom!"

"I think you might be right," he said, and I smiled in relief.

"They've been there so long, I thought they must be one of *my* family's heirlooms. I don't know when you got married, but I was at school thirty years ago, and I remember they were there when I used to visit. My grandfather owned the shop. You could buy them . . . I'll give you a good price."

I wasn't about to buy something that had been stolen from my mum and dad.

"It doesn't matter how long ago they were taken," I said haughtily. "The police will still have the list I wrote out for my father. The case will still be open."

He looked sceptical.

"I don't think too many detectives will be rushing around trying to solve that crime. Although I may be wrong."

"But they're my family's property," I insisted. "That buckle at the top was worn by my grandmother's grandmother. She was in the Crimea with Florence Nightingale.

"The bottom row are my grandad's and the ones with the military medal at the front are my dad's. Look, Amy, there's your great-aunt Daisy's conductor's badge."

I could have given him the whole history of all the other things.

I suppose I got rather excited, but the case had been my parents' most treasured possession.

"That's the kind of people you come from, our Sal," Dad used to say, giving the case its weekly polish. "Brave as lions."

Mr Musgrove's grandson took a bunch of keys out of his pocket and after trying half of them, eventually managed to open the display cabinet, and drew out the treasure chest. He looked at the little white label showing the price, and frowned.

"I don't know why they're priced so high, there's nothing particularly special about them. Just trinkets, really."

"Trinkets?" I exploded. He was talking about something my parents had valued above practically anything!

If I'd used my common sense, I'd have agreed that they *were* only trinkets and got him to let me have them for a pound or two, but as I said, our family had a lot of pride, and I had more than my share.

"Our family gave their blood and years of faithful service for those. They meant something, they're significant. And they were stolen!"

AMY was beginning to look fierce now. After all, it was her family history, too. Musgrove's grandson must have been surprised at being faced with two angry women several generations apart. He had the grace to look ashamed.

"I didn't exactly mean trinkets . . . what I meant to say . . . from a collector's point of view . . . of course, they're priceless as family . . ." He frowned again. "My grandad was an expert. He must have known they'd never sell at that ridiculous price."

He lifted the case carefully and looked at a ticket and number stuck on the bottom, and then gave Amy the case to hold.

"I'll just look and see what grandad wrote in the books. He was one for keeping records. What year did you say?"

He went off. I had a lump in my throat because I could imagine my dad standing next to me proudly looking at the rows of nurse's buckles, the badges and medals, like he had done so often when I was a child, as he told me the stories of each one. I could almost hear his deep voice.

"We enjoy all our cherished freedoms today because they were willing to dedicate their lives to others, Sal. You should be proud."

I looked at Amy clutching her birthright. She wasn't going to give it up any more easily than me. Musgrove's grandson came back lugging a huge ledger that looked positively Dickensian. Amy closed the top of the display case so he could put the book down. He seemed quite excited.

"Look — here's the date, the description of the items, the name of the buyer or seller, and the price advanced, and so on."

He ran his finger down the page of immaculate copperplate writing. It was practically a work of art. His finger stopped at *Mahogany, velvet-lined display case containing medals, buckles, ribbons and badges.*

"But look at this." His finger ran down the end column from the top. "A pound, ten and six, two shillings, fifteen shillings, five bob, and then . . ." His finger reached the treasure chest row and stopped. "Fifty pounds!"

But I wasn't looking at the price; I was looking at the seller's name. Alfred Ernest Faulkner. My dad.

"What's that number?" I asked, pointing to the column next to Dad's name.

"That's the pawn ticket number. But fifty pounds! That must have been unheard of for . . ." He pointed at the treasure chest that his grandad had given so much for. "Well, I mean . . . it isn't exactly the crown jewels, is it? And fifty pounds in those days would have bought . . . I don't know, lots."

Those days of my childhood, right up until my white wedding. I seemed to remember them so well. The marches, soup kitchens, men hanging about street corners waiting for work. None of it seemed so grim because I was young and in love, but they were very tough times. No-one had money to spare. Especially for weddings.

The man frowned.

"But you might be right. Grandad must have bought some stolen goods and covered the expenditure by only entering the medal case."

But that didn't make much sense. No burglar in his right mind would have run off with a wooden box. He'd have just grabbed all the silver medals. And it didn't explain my dad's name as the seller in the ledger.

Then out of the blue I remembered the single pawn ticket in the Gladstone bag, and I knew. The list I'd made out for the police would never have reached them. My dad had known Mr Musgrove all his life. They'd served in India and Flanders together.

Dad would have been too proud to get into debt with a loan. Mum and he must have decided to pawn their most treasured possession to pay for my wedding. It never was stolen. Mr Musgrove had added the wedding gift he'd always promised me, in the price he'd given.

The car crash came before the money was earned to reclaim the pawned family heritage, and George and I had taken my inconsolable mother to the other end of the country.

✳   ✳   ✳   ✳

Amy took the treasure chest to school as part of her history project, and I sit and look at it now in pride of place above the mantelpiece, and wonder if it influenced her decision to serve as a doctor with the UN forces, where she's been awarded a few "trinkets" of her own. ▪

All About Alfie

by Teresa Ashby.

Illustration by Sally Barton.

I TOOK early retirement when Alfie was born. Alfie is my grandson, and I knew Diane would have to go back to work after her maternity leave.

I couldn't bear to think of him going to a nursery, just one little face among many, even though I'm sure they're all very well cared for. So I told Diane I would take care of him while she worked. The way she hugged me when I told her, I knew it was a relief to her, too.

But after a few months, I began to miss my friends, as well as the money I was no longer earning. I'd become rather set in my ways since my children had grown up, and I was used to having money to spend, and going out for lunch with the girls from work.

On the plus side, I lost some weight. It was all that walking, I think, pushing Alfie round in his pushchair, chatting to him, and the occasional sprint for home when it started to rain.

And it was different with a grandchild. I had the time to spend with him that a busy mother sometimes doesn't, and I knew from my own experience

80

that the baby years pass by all too quickly — you have to make the most of them while you can.

I didn't listen when people told me that when my own children were small. I wish I had, but I doubt it would have made any difference. The dusting still had to be done, Tom's shirts still had to be ironed, ready for him to wear to work, and dinners had to be cooked.

I loved Alfie so much that sometimes it almost hurt. I loved the soft pale curves of his cheeks and his perfect little mouth. But it was his eyes that drew people's attention, such big eyes with such dark lashes.

Although I missed the company of adults, I wouldn't have swapped my life for the world.

However, one particular day I was feeling rather hard done by. It sounds silly now, but I'd had a phone call from Jennifer, one of my friends from work. She called to tell me about a theatre trip she'd been on.

Mr Ellison, my old boss, had let the girls from my old department have the whole day off as a reward for some big contract they'd landed and they'd made a day of it, apparently.

"We didn't ask you," Jennifer said blithely, "because we knew you'd be busy with Alfie. How is the dear little fellow? You're so lucky, Pat, we all envy you."

It was my own fault, of course. A couple of times the girls from work had called to ask me out for an evening. But to tell the truth, after a day with Alfie, all I wanted to do was sit down in front of the television with a glass of wine and some cheesy biscuits, and put my feet up, so I'd turned them down.

That Thursday morning I put Alfie in his pushchair and set off for the park, feeling rather sorry for myself. It was about a mile from my house and a pleasant walk in the sunshine.

"Swings, Pat!" Alfie yelled as I turned in through the gates.

The park was deserted. It was school time so the bigger children were in school and it was still quite early, so the young mums would be getting their shopping, and dropping the older ones at school before setting out for the day.

Alfie had taken to calling me Pat since he'd heard my neighbour chatting to me one day. Until then I'd been Nanny.

I didn't mind. I thought it was rather sweet, and I knew he'd go back to calling me Nanny sooner or later.

I parked his pushchair and lifted him out. He ran ahead of me towards the swings, but the toddler swing with its safety rail was broken.

Alfie didn't take the news well.

"I want to go on the swings, Pat," he said earnestly, his chin down as he looked up at me with grave, dark eyes.

Bless him, he thought it was within my power to fix the swing so he could use it.

"I know what we can do," I said, and I sat on one of the proper swings then pulled him on to my lap.

I held the chain with one hand and Alfie with the other, and we swung gently back and forth. I kept one foot in contact with the ground — just in case.

Alfie thought it was wonderful. Even better than the toddler swing. His giggles danced on the air like warm raindrops.

The warden who keeps an eye on things round the play area happened to pass by and I expected to get a telling off, but he smiled and waved.

"You look as if you're having fun. Good for you!"

I must have been mad to hanker after work. This was the life. Out in the sunshine every day, sitting on a swing, what more could I want?

My life now was Peppa Pig and Mr Tumble off the television, and Alfie asleep on my lap in the afternoons while I read my book.

His giggles were like balm, healing me.

We went over to the slide and he slid into my waiting arms, and laughed harder, his cheeks rosy now.

BUT then someone else came into the park. A man was walking in, with a toddler a little older than Alfie running ahead of him. They went straight to the climbing frame. I always kept Alfie well away from it, terrified he'd fall off. We watched the man help the little boy up the ladder and across the rope bridge.

He was having such fun and I could see the longing in Alfie's eyes.

"I'll go on that when I'm bigger, won't I, Pat?" he said, and his little voice sounded so wistful, so longing, that I felt my heart contract.

If only Tom were still here. He could have lifted Alfie on to the frame and been there to catch him. Dear Tom. He'd been gone so long and I missed him so much at times.

If Alfie was sick and tired of hearing me say the words, "When you're bigger," he never said so.

But I could see the longing on his little face. Sometimes "when you're bigger" is just too long to wait.

We wandered over and I tried to help him up on to the frame, but I'm what my daughter jokingly calls vertically challenged, and I knew I couldn't let him climb about on the frame safely.

HERE, I'll keep an eye on him," the man said with a smile. "If you want me to, that is."

He had a nice face. In fact he reminded me a bit of Tom, how I thought he'd have looked if he'd grown older. I always reckoned his hair would go quite white and he'd end up looking distinguished.

I stood next to the climbing frame, almost having kittens as I watched Alfie running across the rope bridge, his little hands grasping the sides. But it was a joy to hear his laughter as he played with the other little boy, and there was reassurance in the man's presence. I felt certain that he would catch Alfie if he missed his footing.

I used to worry a lot less about my own children. I didn't have time to stand over them and watch their every move and they all grew up OK.

"Thank you," I said to the man. "He's enjoying himself up there. It's nice for him to have company of his own age. He's not starting playgroup for a few months yet, but I think he's ready to have friends."

"Samuel's very good," he said. "He gets on well with other children and he likes having someone to play with, too. I think he gets fed up with me."

Soon, but not soon enough for my shattered nerves, the boys decided they'd had enough of the climbing frame and went to play on the slide.

I've always loved watching small children play together, seeing how they interact with each other. It's like watching them take a journey of discovery. I've come to the conclusion that we could learn a lot about ourselves from watching children.

"Shall we sit down while they're playing?" the man asked, and indicated the bench where I'd parked the pushchair.

"My name's Trevor," he said. "And that's Samuel, my grandson."

"Pat," I said. "And my grandson is called Alfie."

"Do you have him all the time?" Trevor asked.

"Yes," I said. "My daughter works."

"Mine, too," he said with a rueful smile. "Things have changed a lot since our children were small, haven't they? But, these days, if they want a roof over their heads, both parents have to work in a lot of cases."

"I suspect my daughter would far rather be a stay-at-home mum," I said. "But she does a great job with him. She's got her priorities right. He always comes first, and sometimes I think the kind of quality time she spends with him is better than all the time I spent with my own — does that make sense?"

He laughed.

"Yes, I think it does. This way they get the best of both worlds. My daughter is a nurse. I took voluntary redundancy in order to look after Samuel. They tried him in a nursery, but he wouldn't settle."

He sighed and we watched the boys taking turns on a little wooden motorbike that was on a spring.

"I have no regrets," he said. "But I do miss the company of adults sometimes. I used to stop off for a drink on my way home with some of the others, and we'd have a game of darts and a little conversation. Now it's all strawberry milkshakes and nursery rhymes."

"Really?" I said. "It's funny, but that's exactly what I miss about working, too — the company. And you're the first person I've admitted that to. It feels wrong, somehow. I have friends who envy me the amount of time I get to spend with Alfie. They hardly see their grandchildren."

"Why does it feel wrong? It's natural to miss people. I bet when you were a young mum you craved adult company."

I laughed. I did! I had forgotten it, but I did. Sometimes after a day spent at home with the children I would feel as if I was going mad.

"You sound like someone who knows. Did your wife tell you that?"

"Every time I got home from work." He laughed. "She used to say I had no idea how it felt to have only a two-year-old to talk to all day."

"I bet she's glad of your help now," I said.

"Well, she would be if she was around," he said. "I lost her a while ago."

So we were both on our own. Well, not entirely on our own. We had our grandsons.

"May I offer him an ice-cream?" Trevor asked.

"Yes," I replied. "Thank you. He'd love that."

We trooped out of the park to the ice-cream van, and Trevor bought us all 99s. Alfie clutched his and couldn't eat it fast enough. Ice-cream ran all over his fingers and down his arms.

Samuel didn't seem to be faring much better.

But I haven't had five children and a grandson without learning a thing or

84

Nash Point, Glamorgan, Wales

IT was while on a recent trip to Wales that my husband and I stopped at Nash Point. Having checked ahead, we were lucky enough to be able to go on a guided tour of the building. It really captured my imagination, seeing and hearing how the lighthouse keeper would have gone about his daily business of making sure that vessels at sea were safely kept away from the rocky shoreline. What a fascinating existence!

It does seem a shame that none of them are manned any more, but a benefit to us, as we learned that the keeper's cottages are available as holiday accommodation — maybe next time!

To cap it all, we heard a sounding of the mighty foghorn before we left to continue our journey through this beautiful part of Britain.

— Mrs J.D., Birmingham.

J. CAMPBELL KERR.

two, and I whipped a packet of baby wipes out of my bag.

I swiftly cleaned the boys and showed them how to lick round the edges of the cone to stop the ice-cream dripping. They grinned grateful, white, ice-creamy smiles at me.

"You're quite an expert," Trevor said. "I always forget things like baby wipes."

"It helps having a handbag the size of a small suitcase," I said. "Men's pockets don't lend themselves to carrying such things."

"They certainly don't." He laughed.

We sat on the grass and talked, and it occurred to me that I'd got the adult company I'd been yearning for at last, and what did we talk about? Our grandchildren!

But it was a long time since I'd laughed so much — and not just because Mr Tumble had done something funny on the television.

THE afternoon flew by. The boys had such fun and so did I. I came to realise that Alfie really is the most important person in my life right now, and I wouldn't change it for the world.

"Gracious," Trevor said. "Is that the time? Stella will be finishing her shift soon and coming to fetch Samuel."

He called Samuel over, borrowed a baby wipe to give him a quick once over, then, grasping his hand, began to head for his car.

Alfie held my hand and waved to them, his thumb stuck in his mouth, then Trevor stopped.

"Are you coming to the park tomorrow?" he called out.

"Yes," I said. "If it's nice."

"See you then!" he called out and gave us a cheery wave.

"Hear that, Alfie?" I said. "You'll be able to play with Samuel tomorrow, too."

"Yay!" He cheered.

We skipped home. Alfie didn't want to go in his pushchair and I pushed it with one hand and held his hand with the other.

Diane was working a half-day today and it was almost time for her to pick him up. We just had time for a drink and a biscuit before she arrived.

Then, as we packed his things into his bag, he flung his arms round my neck, and squeezed so tight I could barely breathe.

"I've had such a lovely time, Nanny," he said.

Oh, I was Nanny again. I much preferred it. It was a title I felt I'd worked hard for, and earned.

"So have I, sweetheart." I squeezed him tight. "So have I."

And more wonderful times were still to come. The best days of my life so far. Watching my gorgeous little grandson grow up, I felt like the luckiest woman in the world. ∎

IT was a relief to escape to the attic, away from the Luxbridge Mothers' Union and Mrs Bloomsbury-Chatwyn ruling the roost in Sienna's own sitting-room. The wretched woman's strident tones had followed her every step of the way up here.

Of course they must put on a party for the dear little children. It was Coronation Day. The whole country would be partying!

Tea cups clinked. Sienna imagined a collective sigh of browbeaten sensibilities. She knew her mothers would have preferred to celebrate the occasion in some other, less noisy way.

She swayed, slightly out of breath, pushing back the hair flopping down over her high forehead indicating the deeply sensible person everyone knew

by Sam Horsley.

Illustration by David Axtell.

Treasures In The Attic

her for. They didn't know her as well as they thought! Up here in the rectory attic, so many occasions when she hadn't been sensible sprang easily to mind.

A large rectangle of sunlight splayed through the dormer window her father had installed when they'd first arrived in the village and this tiny space had been designated her bedroom. What a refuge it had been. What a hotchpotch of odds and ends of a life it was now.

Hats, suitcases, her father's old Gladstone bag, the box camera with which he'd marked her childhood. Delighted, her gaze settled on the bunting she'd just assured Mrs Bloomsbury-Chatwyn was still up here, shoved under a chair as if the person stowing it there had wanted to forget the war, the end of which had signalled its last time in use.

A cuckoo clock balanced precariously on a pile of old packing cases. A present from a grateful parishioner, it used to hang in the hall until Gerald, her father, had tired of it. Fumbling, her fingers grown oddly clumsy, she opened up the little door at the front and pulled out a bundle of envelopes. The last place anyone would expect to discover such bounty, or so she'd thought when she'd hidden them here. How many years ago now?

How unmindful she was of her ladies downstairs. Slowly, deliciously, she picked up the first and extracted the single sheet of paper inside. Gregory's eager and untidy scrawl or Roland's neat and measured script? The writing was fading already.

Mrs Bloomsbury-Chatwyn's voice dimmed, grew silent. Sienna sank down into a chair, her mind miles away at the start of it all . . .

"MISSED me?" Gregory laughed wickedly.

Sienna spun round, milk-pan in hand, to see him framed in the rectory doorway, his dark tumbling hair tinged with autumn fire. It was early evening and warm, the door through from the garden flung wide. Since Chamberlain had declared the country at war, the weather had been remarkable.

"Where've you been?" Roland asked quietly.

They both knew Gregory's disappearance had meant something. They'd just been discussing it.

"Manchester!" he cried, confirming what Roland had already daringly suggested, bouncing in and throwing his cap on the table. "I'm signed up. RAF Pilot — under training. I've to report to Baddacombe, Sunday week."

"Gregory, you haven't . . ."

"Why shouldn't I?" he answered coolly. "I have to do something. I shall put in for fighter training, too, if they'll have me. I'd rather have a choice now than wait until I'm called up. Any of that cocoa going, Sien? I'm parched."

"I'm pleased for you, old man. Congratulations." Roland, ever generous, shook his friend's hand, though Sienna sensed the news must have thrown him, too.

Amid the ensuing excitement, the dog barking, her father bustling in to add his effusions, the extra milk boiling and spilling over, the little party finally calmed down.

"Have you thought what you'll do, Roly?" Gregory finished his cocoa, watching his friends across the table.

The three of them together. It had been so ever since Sienna had first arrived in the village, an untidy girl with pigtails, knowing no-one and grateful for the friendship the two boys offered.

Roland, the son of a gentleman farmer, educated at Eton and down for Oxford, was being brought up with the proverbial silver spoon in his mouth. Gregory, on the other hand, eked out a precarious existence with his farm worker father on the edges of the Marchmain Estate.

He had brains, good looks, charm — too much for anyone. Fred Marchmain, Roland's father, had recognised the potential in the boy and paid his fees at the local grammar school. Everyone knew Gregory would get on. But so far, so fast? He was leaving them behind, even Roland. Why did the fact tug so at Sienna's heart-strings?

Roland's large, handsome face had dropped. He'd been agonising for weeks over what he ought to do.

"I'll defer Oxford, of course," he muttered, ignoring Gregory's nod of approval. "Dad's not well. He wants me to stay on, even if I'm not sure . . ." He'd always wanted to do the most good he could, unlike Gregory, who just wanted to get on.

"I think you should, Roly. It's a reserved occupation. Farmers will be desperately needed."

Sienna couldn't bear for both her friends to go. Selfish, she knew, but it would drive her mad to be stuck in the rectory with only her father for company.

She was aware of a sudden tension.

"But surely you want to fight?" Gregory sounded perplexed.

"I'm not sure I do," Roland confessed unhappily, staring down into his cocoa. "I just wish we'd explored all the options. Surely fighting should be the last resort?"

"How can you negotiate with a madman like Hitler?"

"I'm not saying I have any answers." He was confused and unhappy. The world was at war. They were growing up too fast.

"Don't let's fall out," Sienna implored, looking quickly from one to the other.

✳   ✳   ✳   ✳

From Baddacombe, Gregory wrote regular, jokey letters telling her how training was going. She looked forward to their arrival; watching for the postman, running out as soon as she heard the latch on the gate. At last one

89

arrived bearing the wonderful news — he'd been given leave.

An oddly shorn Gregory arrived, dashing in RAF uniform, holding them captive with all his exploits. He loved flying. He was going to make a go of this.

Roland regarded him with his usual brotherly affection, but how did this new Gregory make Sienna feel? Things had changed in a way she hadn't expected.

His feet scarcely touched base before he was off again. Letters arrived thick and fast, telling her nothing except that life was wonderful and the war was affording him so many opportunities. He always sent his love. Was it only a warm expression towards an old and valued friend? Why did she even give it a second thought? It was only typical Gregory.

He passed training and transferred to an air-base on the coast. To Sienna's horror, he was accepted for fighter training.

Garden Glories!

IF there's a corner of your patio that could do with brightening up, you'll love Californian Lilac. One of many different ceanothus varieties, the Thyrsiflorus Var Repens is worth mentioning for its beautiful steel blue flower clusters. It's also a dwarf variety that won't overpower the pot or grow higher than one metre.

Creeping blueblossom (Californian Lilac) is a low growing and spreading evergreen shrub with glossy mid-green leaves, which bears true blue flower clusters. Grow in fertile, well-drained soil in full sun. Make sure you shelter your ceanothus from cold drying winds, though, as this will damage the leaves in winter.

At home, Roland was assigned a group of land-girls. Sienna threw herself into life at the vicarage and joined the WVS. The war began to gather pace. Ration books. Evacuees. The debacle at Dunkirk shattered their conviction that it would soon be over.

FOLLOWING Lord Beaverbrook's appeal for aluminium for Spitfires, and feeling more effort was needed on her part, she helped to collect the mountains of pots and pans to build one.

"Odd if Gregory gets to fly the one made from these," she mused.

Roland had just dumped a box of saucepans on the table. He looked drawn and tired. Things were difficult on the farm.

"Let's just hope he's all right," he responded.

"He can tell us himself. He's home on leave the day after tomorrow." She laughed, flinging her arms around him. "He's written. I was saving it up as a surprise!"

"Don't, Sien!" To her bewilderment, he pulled her arms away. She backed away, confused.

"I thought you'd be pleased . . ."

90

New branches are soft and drooping and flowers appear in warmer days of late spring. As it will flower right through the summer, this is a very attractive plant and one that you're sure to like!

There was an odd expression on his face.

"You like Greg, don't you? I mean, more than me?"

"We're friends, aren't we?" she cried, confused. Kind, gentle Roland, so slow to temper. Why was he looking so cross? Her question was soon answered. Words she didn't want to hear were tumbling from his lips, quietly, relentlessly, as if he'd been saving them up and couldn't hold them in any longer.

"Don't you realise how I feel about you?" he cried angrily. "I love you. I've always loved you! Oh, Sienna, please don't tell me I've left it too late. I mean, do you . . . could you . . . have any feelings for me?"

"I have feelings for you both," she blustered, trying to cover an awkward pause. "In a sisterly way."

Even as she said it, she knew it wasn't true. She dwelled on Gregory far more than she ever used to do. But did that mean she felt more for him than she ought and more than she felt for Roland? A warm little glow sprang up inside at thoughts of Gregory.

Had Roland guessed? His hand moved upwards, caressing her cheek. She stepped quickly away, out of his reach, too overcome to think anything other than it wasn't what she wanted.

"I shouldn't have said anything. Forgive me." His hand dropped away. "Forget it. You know what I'm like."

She did. Sensitive. Thoughtful. Feeling everything too much. She'd handled it badly.

"Let's just look forward to Gregory's return." Her voice was calm, her heart beating too fast. Words easily spoken would be hard to forget. Something had changed between them.

GREGORY had a forty-eight-hour pass. Sienna concentrated her efforts on getting through the next day, which included a WVS meeting followed by an afternoon settling a group of Polish emigrés into new digs in the village.

The following morning was fine, a summer's morning like any other, except it wasn't any other. Gregory was coming home and she couldn't contain her excitement. When had her feelings changed?

Using some of his precious petrol ration, Roland was driving them to the station to meet Gregory's train. When his truck pulled up, she ran to the door to greet him.

"Is everything all right?" she demanded eagerly, surprised to see him looking so worried. Was he still upset?

He took her arm and led her gently back into the kitchen. There was something else. A pain sprang up, threatening to overwhelm her.

"It's Gregory, isn't it? Roland, for goodness' sake, tell me!"

He look a deep breath.

"Ted's had a telegram. His plane got into a spot of bother with a Messerschmitt over the Channel. He limped back to base and crash-landed. I'm not sure how badly he's hurt."

* * * *

They travelled on too-slow trains and badly timed connections, arriving weary and distraught at the bustling cottage hospital near to the air-base long after visiting time was over. A sympathetic nurse ushered them into the ward.

"Not long, mind. Sister'll have my guts for garters if she knows I've let you in."

Both Greg's legs were broken and suspended in pulleys; his right arm, nursing a broken collar-bone, hung in a sling. Two broken ribs and a large bump on his forehead completed the damage. He'd been miraculously lucky. A charmed life, as always.

He lay back against the pillow, trying to look sorry for himself, but his eyes glittered, fastening on Sienna greedily.

"I thought you'd never get here."

Some of Sienna's tension relaxed. He'd be all right. She'd look after him. Her father would have to see to himself for a while.

A KIND WVS lady put them up for the night and the following day she found herself digs near the hospital. Roland had to get back to the estate. It was harvest time and there was too much to do.

"Don't worry. I'll make sure and take care of both of us," Sienna urged, wanting to hug him and knowing it wasn't a good idea.

"Blasted Jerry! I'd like to get my hands on the one who did this," Roland snarled, angrier on Gregory's behalf than she'd ever seen him. He hurried off to catch his train, abandoning Sienna to her twice-daily visits to the hospital, encouraging, cajoling and prodding the reluctant invalid to a full recovery.

One wonderful morning, several trying weeks later, he was already up and waiting for her in the day room where one of his army of besotted nurses had wheeled him, an idiotic smile plastered on his face. The sun shone through the large bay window and on to his curls which had grown again, wild as ever.

"The plaster on my left leg's off tomorrow!" He beamed happily, grabbing her hand. "I'm starting physiotherapy. Another couple of months and I'll be passed fit for flying again."

"Gregory, that's wonderful!"

It was, wasn't it? Then what was tearing at her heart? That next time he might not be so lucky?

His grip on her hand tightened. She sank down into the chair next to him, not sure if she ought to leave it there. He was stroking it almost absent-mindedly, sending shivers tingling up her spine.

"I couldn't have got through this without you, Sien. You must know how I feel about you?"

The words she'd dreamed of hearing. They were wrong, or at least too late. Gently she disengaged her hand.

"Greg, this isn't the time," she said.

"But I love you."

"You think you do." How could she keep her voice so cool when he'd thrown her into such confusion?

He leaned back, a thwarted child, watching her quizzically.

"It's Roland, isn't it!" he demanded crossly.

"In a way," she prevaricated, then decided she'd have to tell him. "He thinks he loves me."

She faltered, upset by his petulant expression.

"Can't you see, Greg? You and I . . . How could we? It would hurt him terribly!"

"It doesn't change the way I feel."

"What else can we do?"

"Everything!" The young man frowned. "He's big enough. He'll get over it."

Was all fair in love and war?

"Let's at least wait until the end of things," she implored.

UNABLE to shake off the feeling she was running away, she fled back home where another shock awaited. A man in an ill-fitting Army uniform, cap set at a determined angle, strode down the platform to meet her train.

"Roland?"

The man grinned sheepishly, reaching for her hand, gripping it awkwardly, instantly her old and cherished friend.

"Lucky our trains have crossed. I report to Aldershot for basic training this afternoon."

"But the farm . . . Roland, you don't believe in war."

"Now we've got the land-girls, Dad can just about manage. I was only fudging things, Sienna. If it took Greg's being shot down to show me sometimes fighting's the only way, then so be it."

A new Roland. Not much of a soldier but a determined one, wanting to do his bit to bring this unhappy period in the world's history to a close. Should she tell him how she felt about Gregory? It seemed dishonest not to say something.

"Roland . . . Gregory and I —"

"Ssshh! Don't tell me. I don't want to know." He laid a finger against her lips then leaned forward and kissed her, a gentle kiss, devoid of passion. Had she imagined his declaration of love?

SHE returned to the rectory and tried to pick up the threads of her life as, in quick succession, letters arrived; Gregory's full of his recovery and a hastily arranged date with the RAF Medical Board; then a letter from Roland, joking of his growing horror of square bashing. Underneath she sensed steely determination.

I miss you, Sienna, he concluded, sending all his love.

His unexpected war continued. He sailed to Greece to join his unit and if he was given leave, he never came home to spend it.

Have you made your mind up yet? Gregory wrote.

Something had to be done. Gregory was obviously of a like mind, too. One bright winter's morning, to Sienna's joy, he turned up at the vicarage. The hospital had given him the all-clear, and, wanting to surprise her, he'd taken the overnight train.

"Sienna, darling. I can't believe how much I've missed you!"

Greg stood in the kitchen, the charming smile he turned on so easily flashing in her direction, turning her knees to water.

She'd been making cakes for the ladies' union. Powdered milk, eggs, too little flour. Her hands were trembling. He looked so handsome. He'd been through so much. She couldn't think of Roland now.

She dusted her hands, her heart overflowing as, arms wide, Gregory strode across the kitchen.

The shrill ring of the telephone in the hall stopped him in his tracks. Pulling a resigned face, Sienna went through to answer it. Her face, when she returned, was drained of colour.

"Fred's had a telegram. Roly's unit's been involved in action. He's posted missing . . ."

* * * *

Even now she remembered that dreadful time; Gregory's white face, her father wonderfully taking charge and phoning anyone and everyone from whom he might glean the slightest sliver of information.

Dennis Hardley.

Furry Fred

I HAD a caterpillar pet,
  His name was Furry Fred,
I woke him every morning
And at night put him to bed.
He led the life of Riley,
Basking in the sun all day,
And he gave the firm impression
That he was here to stay.
I fed him on fresh lettuce leaves
With beads of dew to sup,
So there's no doubt I pampered him,
Whilst he was growing up.
Yet he still played a trick on me,
I really don't know why,
For no-one could have cared for him
More fervently than I.
But he turned into a chrysalis,
Then grew some fairy wings,
And when I think about it,
The memory still stings.
He flew without a backward glance,
My now ex-furry pet,
And after all the things I've done,
That's all the thanks I get!

— *Brian H. Gent.*

It was five long days, the longest in her life, before news came through that Roland was slightly wounded and a prisoner of war. The letter the Red Cross had so wonderfully delivered trembled in Sienna's hand. How thankful the whole village had been that, for Roland, the war was finally over.

ARLING, whatever are you doing? The ladies . . . Mrs Bloomsbury-Chatwyn. I've been sent up to winkle you out. Wretched woman nearly came up here herself!"

Her husband's head, his voice full of laughter and reduced to a theatrical stage whisper, appeared through the opening. He scrambled up, a smile on his handsome face that, even after all these years, still had the power to move her.

Sienna turned, spilling the letters on to her lap, her eyes bright with unexpected tears. It had been so long ago. They'd been through so much.

"I found these. Oh, but, darling, it has taken me back!"

He crouched down and gathered letters, discarded envelopes, sifting them with his large, capable hands, his face over its clerical collar breaking into a wide smile of wonder. Stirring memories, too?

"I'd never realised you'd kept them. What a pair of senseless young idiots we were." All at once the banter in his voice disappeared. "I've never understood, no matter how many times you've tried to explain. Why me, darling? I was nothing compared with Gregory . . ."

Gregory . . . whose first absence had made her heart grow fonder than it ought. It had been nothing compared to how she'd felt when she'd discovered her darling Roland in the hands of the German Army.

She leaned forward and stilled his lips with a kiss, still perplexed that it had taken her so long to work it out. How could she *not* have chosen Roland, a man who considered all sides of a problem before he made up his mind and yet was unafraid to admit himself wrong and change it back? A loyal, steadfast friend who valued friendship beyond material gain. A man who wanted to do the best he could with his life, hence, after the war, his putting Ted Standing in charge as manager of the Marchmain Estate, so that he himself could train for the church and the chance to do good, which was all he'd ever wanted.

When Sienna's father had so sadly passed away, it had seemed fate they should come back here where it had all started.

Gregory was no longer around. He was making such a wonderful success of his life, putting all he'd learned in the RAF to huge commercial success in the freight cargo business, and was well on his way to becoming a millionaire.

"Yoohoo! Anyone up there? Shall I come up?"

Mrs Bloomsbury-Chatwyn's voice floated up the stairs. They broke away, laughing.

"You're everything to me, darling," Sienna whispered, heart bursting because she knew it was so. ■

Boys Will Be Boys

by Mary Kettlewell.

Illustration by Andy Walker.

"WHAT'S that?"
Clive Jamieson tugged at his younger brother's grey flannel shorts.
"Where? Let's have a look."
Ten-year-old Jem elbowed him aside and peered through the missing

97

fence palings. A curious sight met his eyes. A machine with two large black wheels, and a small front one attached to a T-shaped steering arm, was slowly emerging from the woodshed next door.

Pushing the contraption was an elderly lady in a grey skirt, grey coat and even greyer felt hat.

"She looks a dragon," Clive whispered. "Worse than Miss Thornby at school."

"Look at the old boy steering. He must be all of a hundred."

He was muffled in a thick great-coat with a long woollen scarf wrapped round his neck. He had a long grey beard, a brown trilby hat and between his clenched teeth was a pipe.

They watched, eyes agog, as the machine proceeded at a dignified pace between the flower-beds and out into the lane. Clive had a distant look in his eyes.

"I bet she can travel, once you get her going."

"It's like that Roman chariot in the Robert Mitchum film."

A voice called from the kitchen window.

"Jem! Clive! Tea's ready. Don't forget to wash your hands."

＊　　＊　　＊　　＊

Jem took a mouthful of corned-beef pie and chewed fiercely.

"We saw a chariot next door and an old man with a beard."

"There was a woman pushing it. A prune-face, like Miss Thornby."

"That's quite enough, boys. And don't talk with your mouths full."

Dorothy, their mother, tried to keep the smile from her face.

"I gather he's called Mr Outhwaite. Miss Frew, the vicar's sister, takes him out most afternoons."

"What's that thing he's sitting in?" Jem asked.

"It's a bath chair. It belongs to the parish, and it's for the use of elderly people who can't walk. The vicar looks after it."

"Can we have a go in it, Mum?"

"I can't hardly walk myself — I've grazed my knee on my bike pedal," Jem said, always quick off the mark.

Their mother sighed. Boys! They were all the same — up to all sorts.

Dorothy dished out healthy portions of plum duff and turned to the sink.

It had been a wrench leaving the village where she'd lived all her life, but Roy had been over the moon at the prospect of his promotion.

"It's on a hop farm at Little Beckenham, Dorothy. A cottage to go with it, and a pound a week rise. It's a heaven-sent opportunity."

Boxford Cottage had seemed ideal.

98

Reasonable rent, close to the village shop and a ten-minute walk from the school. But she missed her friends, and sometimes Roy would be out soon after first light and not back till late.

IT was the weekend, and two pairs of eyes were looking through the palings in Mr Outhwaite's creosoted fence.

"She doesn't seem to come on a Saturday, Clive."

"There's no door on the shed, either. I can see the front wheel sticking out."

"There's a thick hedge in front of Mr Outhwaite's window. He can't see the path. Shall we?"

"What if he comes out?"

"He can't, stupid. His legs are bad."

They slipped through a hole in the hedge and crouched low behind the screen of yew. The shed smelled of drying onions and dust. The chariot stood there in all its splendour, a tartan cushion resting on the seat.

Very quietly, they backed it out and pushed it away from the house.

"You go first." Clive heaved on the handles.

The bath chair wobbled, steadied, and then began to run smoothly down the path, Jem steering it with the T-shaped handle.

All went well for twenty minutes, until they recalled the Roman centurion in the film.

"Let's try racing it!"

Away they went, Clive pushing like fury. Jem swung the wheel hard round to avoid a protruding stone from the rockery and the front wheel, now sideways on, buckled under the strain. The machine tipped over, depositing Jem at the foot of an apple tree. He sprawled face-down amongst the windfalls.

"Now you've done it!"

"It's your fault for turning the wheel too far."

They guiltily pushed the crippled machine back into the shed and covered it with the white dustsheet.

"Don't tell Mum. She'll give us a clip."

"Dad will go mad if he finds out."

The secret was short-lived. Dorothy knew there was something wrong at teatime. When two ten- and eleven-year-old boys say they aren't hungry, a mother's ears prick up.

"Have you two been up to mischief? And how did you get those grazed knees, Jem?"

There was silence for a full minute. Then Jem could hold back no longer.

"We've wrecked Mr Outhwaite's chariot, Mum."

Clive stared at his untouched mashed potato.

"We took the corner too fast and it crashed."

Dorothy was almost lost for words. Here she was, trying to settle into a new village and keep on friendly terms with the neighbours, and they'd thrown a fly into the ointment already. No, a hornet, more like.

"What's your father going to say, that's what I'd like to know?" she muttered darkly.

Five minutes later, they found out. Roy came in smelling of hops, his hands stained brown, and hair full of dust. He took one look at the boys' glum faces and Dorothy's frown.

"What's up?"

"You'd best tell your father, boys."

"We've crashed Mr Outhwaite's chariot, Dad."

"The wheel got buckled. Sorry."

Roy was a good father and he loved his boys, but there were limits.

"We've been in the village barely five minutes and you two are behaving like a pair of hooligans! You deserve a good clip round the ear!" he bellowed.

Dorothy slapped her bread dough on to the worktop.

"What are we going to do, Roy?"

"We? It's what *they* are going to do that matters, and they're going to go round this minute and own up. Tell Mr Outhwaite you're sorry."

"And the vicar?" Dorothy kneaded the dough. "He'll have to be told."

"He will and all. Now get out of my sight, you two."

IT was a very chastened and fearful pair of boys who knocked on Mr Outhwaite's door.

"He'll murder us."

"Get us locked up in gaol, more likely."

They tapped again. Nothing. They knocked louder. Then a voice bellowed out.

"If that's the fishman, come on in. How do you think I can get to the door with my legs?"

Gingerly, they stepped inside. The house smelled of leather and pipe tobacco. Mr Outhwaite looked terrifying.

"Who are you?"

"Jem and Clive from next door, sir."

"Speak up, boy."

"From next door. Me and my brother — we moved in last week."

"Hmm, I thought you were the fishman. I suppose you've kicked a football over and want permission to get it back?"

Clive hung his head.

"Worse, sir."

"We've crashed your chariot, Mr Outhwaite."

There was a long silence broken only by the sizzle of a pipe.

"Trespassing and criminal damage, eh? What do you think you were playing at?"

"Racing it, sir."

"And the front wheel buckled when we steered too hard."

He picked up a glass ashtray and for a terrible moment they thought he was

Folkestone, Kent, England

*H*OW lovely to see Folkestone on the cover. For me, the painting perfectly captures the colourful waterfront, where my husband and I have spent so many lovely holidays.

Coming from the hustle and bustle of London, we always looked forward to our time spent in Folkestone. Sunny days on the seafront listening to the gentle clinking of the boats in the harbour; short walks in the glorious countryside of the nearby North Downs, and my husband always enjoyed a trip to the Battle Of Britain museum at nearby Hawkinge.

We always seemed to get good weather when we were there, so it made a charming break from our busy London lives!

— *Mrs E.B., London.*

J. CAMPBELL KERR.

going to hurl it at them. His voice was gruff.

"The Egyptians pursued them, all Pharaoh's horses and chariots and his horsemen and his army, and overtook them."

"What did you say, sir?"

"Exodus, fourteen. But never mind that. You deserve a good horse-whipping, do you understand?"

"Yes, sir."

"Pocket money being stopped. Banished to your rooms for a month."

"Yes, sir."

Suddenly Mr Outhwaite burst out into a peal of laughter, his beard shaking with the sound. They stared, mouths open.

"Racing? You young whippersnappers! It reminds me of when we used to play up at the ruined castle — firing bows and arrows, locking up prisoners in dungeons. We scrumped apples one day, and the bobby chased us. Crashed our bikes in the lane, apples rolling about all over the place. My, what a clout that copper gave us . . ."

"We're really sorry, sir."

"And so you should be."

"Our dad says we've got to tell the vicar."

"The vicar? It's Ted Shorter, the blacksmith, that we need. He owes me a favour. I gave him a set of sledgehammers when I retired."

"But our dad will —"

"Think you're making up a tale? Tell him to come round. I'll put him right. Most lads would have spun a yarn — blamed all and sundry. You've been honest, and I like that."

They walked out feeling two feet taller.

✳   ✳   ✳   ✳

"Mr Outhwaite wants a word, Dad."

"I'm not surprised," Roy muttered. "He'll be wanting me to pay for the damage."

Ten minutes later he was back.

"You two have got off lightly. The blacksmith says he can sort it out. But no more tomfoolery — all right?"

"There won't be, Dad."

"Honest."

IT had been Dorothy's idea.

"I'll make him a blackberry and apple pie. He's been so good to take it all so well."

The boys carried it across the next morning.

"You two again, eh? Broken the fence playing cricket, I suppose?"

"No, Mr Outhwaite, we've brought you one of Mum's pies."

"Corned beef?"

"Blackberry and apple. Cream to go with it."

His face seemed to be looking less fierce.

"My favourite. You tell your mother she's very kind. Now I've something to show *you*."

He struggled to his feet and they tensed.

"All right, all right, I'm not such a wreck that I can't walk across the room."

Slowly they followed him across the room to a door, which he opened, gesturing to them to move inside. It was like a dream. The space was entirely filled with model railway tracks, engines, points and platforms. Crowds of passengers thronged the concourse. Guards waved miniature green flags and a coal train waited in the sidings beneath a bank of switches. Mr Outhwaite glanced at his watch.

"The four-twenty-two King's Cross to Aberdeen is due to depart in two minutes. Go on, lads — second switch on the top row. That's it. Now move that lever over and let the goods train out, Jem. Slowly, now. There. She's away."

They stayed so long that, having completely lost track of time, their father turned up looking for them. Within two minutes he was well and truly hooked.

"Are you a railwayman, Mr Outhwaite?"

"Aye. Forty-six years. Started out as a stoker and worked my way up to driver."

Three sets of eyes stared enviously.

"Did you drive —"

"The Flying Scotsman? No, but I took the boat train down to Folkestone many a time. Schools class, mostly. Repton, Christ's Hospital, Ardingly. Lovely locomotives."

DUSK was falling when the menfolk finally returned home from next door.

"Where in the world have you been?" Dorothy asked.

"Mr Outhwaite's got millions of trains, Mum."

"He worked on them all."

Roy's eyes lit up.

"Guess what? We nearly collided the Penzance express with a goods train on the fast down line."

Dorothy kissed him affectionately.

"Roy, you great big baby!"

Then she ruffled the boys' hair.

"It's high time you lot had your dinner."

*   *   *   *

Just like the pie, it was Dorothy who first came up with the idea again.

"We'll have a birthday party for Mr Outhwaite. Seventy-nine and all on his own — it can't be any fun for the old boy."

She spent the whole weekend baking. Rock buns, a Victoria sponge, flapjacks, macaroons and an iced cake with seven blue and nine red candles. She called in to him as soon as the boys had left for school.

"We'd all like you to come round for a birthday tea, Mr Outhwaite. If you'd care to . . ."

Mr Outhwaite cracked a joke, but she had a shrewd suspicion it was to hide his true feelings.

"Hmm, I thought you'd come round to complain that the washing on the line was reeking of pipe baccy."

"We could wheel you over to our place in the bath chair," she said softly.

She was certain she caught a sparkle of moistness in his eyes.

"It's ten years gone since I lost my Betty, and I haven't had a birthday party since. There doesn't seem to be much point, not when you're on your own with no family close by." Then he chuckled and returned to his old gruff self.

"But don't expect me to be dressing up like some shop dummy."

"You're fine as you are, Mr Outhwaite. I get a little lonely at home during the day, so it's nice to have someone to talk to."

Mr Outhwaite puffed out a thick cloud of smoke, and managed an answer, even though his voice felt unsteady.

"You've picked a bad-tempered old codger with me, my dear."

"Go on with you," she replied, patting him on the arm. "You're all bluster on top and soft as a marshmallow inside."

The two boys had their own idea as to a birthday present. A crazy one, as you'd expect from a couple of chariot-wreckers.

"We can't, it's too steep."

"We could, if Dad pushed and we pulled."

They pestered their father the minute he came in.

"We need you to push, Dad."

"It'll be too heavy for us."

"Go on, Dad. He said he'd never see it again."

"It would be the best birthday present ever."

Roy poured out a bottle of brown ale and took a long pull.

"What'll you two lads come up with next? Playing bumper cars in a couple of steamrollers, I don't doubt!"

Five more minutes of arm-twisting, and they had him on their side, however reluctantly.

THE day of Mr Outhwaite's seventy-ninth dawned bright and sunny.

"Happy birthday, Mr Outhwaite! We're taking you up to the old castle."

"In the racing chariot!"

Roy stepped forward with a grin on his face.

"Don't worry, I'm acting as emergency brake and auxiliary horsepower."

The old man began to shake with delighted laughter.

"The castle, lads? You'll never do it. It's steeper than Everest, that lane."

But they did, the two boys hauling on ropes attached to the frame, with Roy pushing from behind.

It was a tough climb, and their muscles were on fire by the time they breasted the knoll. Round the ruins they went, Mr Outhwaite giving a running commentary.

"That's where we fired bows and arrows — through those slits up there."

He pointed to a dank flight of stone steps.

"Dungeons with rats, chains and bread and water. You see that ditch? We had a drawbridge there, made from planks torn off Farmer Howland's barn when his back was turned."

Behind the old tower was an orchard of stunted apple trees, lichen-covered and bare-branched.

"We scrumped some of those apples, and over there by the lane is where we crashed our bikes and got a walloping from the constable."

Then it was back home for a scrumptious birthday tea. Dorothy cut him a slice of cake after he'd huffed out the candles, and set it in front of him with a glass of sweet sherry.

"Seventy-nine," he said, "and I feel like a young lad of thirteen again."

That was enough for everyone to know that he'd had an unforgettable day.

MR OUTHWAITE has now become so much a part of the Jamieson family that you couldn't imagine it without him.

Every Saturday, the boys push him along the lane in the bath chair. No chariot racing, just a nice trip into the countryside. Just occasionally he'll take a corner a little too sharply.

"Just to keep the spirit of adventure alive," as he puts it. Sunday lunch-time sees him coming over to share the lamb and mint sauce and sherry trifle.

As for Roy, he seems to spend half his spare time checking Mr Outhwaite's boiler and bringing in the coke, so he says. If you ask Dorothy, she'd reckon they were rerouting the goods train to Rhondda steelworks and trying to get the 11:17 out of Penzance and up to Fort William on time.

And Dorothy? Every time she has a baking session, she cooks a few extras and takes them in.

As Mr Outhwaite said himself after one Sunday lunch, when he'd struck up his pipe outside, "If it wasn't such a darned mouthful, I think I'd be calling myself Mr Jacob Outhwaite-Jamieson, that I would!" ■

Hopping Mad

by Carolyn Williamson.

THE sun was warm on her bare arms, welcome after the rainy spring. Millie tended her flourishing allotment with enthusiasm and tender pride, but hoeing was hard work and she was more than happy to take a break when Cal staggered over from the adjoining plot clutching his prize pet for her inspection and, Millie guessed, fulsome admiration.

"This is Barnaby and that's Britney over in the cage." Cal hugged the creature, his skinny eight-year-old arms barely able to carry it.

Millie leaned on her hoe and brushed the hair out of her eyes.

"Well, hello, Barnaby." She scratched gently behind its ears. "You're a very fine rabbit." He was indeed — enormous, fluffy and lop-eared with an endearing bunny face.

Cal buried his fingers in the thick, soft fur.

"Dad brought them over in the car; they didn't mind a bit. I don't think rabbits get carsick. I sat in the back with them in case they got frightened, though. I hope they like it here."

He looked back at the big, airy shed and sighed.

"I hope they won't get lonely at night. Britney's still got a horrible bite on her leg. That's why I can't get her out to show you."

"It's only for a few days, though, isn't it; until your dad builds a better run for them at home."

Millie had heard the whole story from Cal — how Barnaby and Britney had been attacked by next-door's rescue cat, a half-wild tom, and how Cal's dad had thrown himself on the allotment committee's mercy ("strictly no livestock"), pleading to keep the rabbits on his allotment until he could build a safe, reinforced home for them.

"They'll be much safer here in the meantime, and you can see them every

Illustration by Richard Eraut.

day," Millie assured him.

"I've got to come and feed them and Dad says I can let them out for a hop as long as I look after them carefully. He's going to make a run for them; he's just getting some wire mesh." Cal hugged the rabbit closer.

"Hi. I see you've met Barnaby." Cal's dad, Nathan, ambled up — lean, tanned and looking, Millie thought, very presentable in a blue shirt and clean jeans instead of the usual jumble-sale collection that was *de rigueur* amongst allotment folk.

Millie looked down at her own sagging, ripped and dirt-spattered T-shirt and jeans and mud-caked wellies and sighed regretfully.

"He's gorgeous," she said wistfully, then flushed a little. "Barnaby, I mean. And Britney, though we haven't been formally introduced yet." She winked at Cal who smiled back.

"You don't mind having them next to your plot?" Nathan asked.

"Not at all — as long as they can't get out, and I'm sure they won't." Millie tickled Barnaby's ear again. "An allotment must look like an all-you-can-eat buffet to a rabbit," she mused.

"They'll be in their cages in the shed," Nathan assured her. "Houdini couldn't get out of there, never mind fat old Barnaby." He smiled fondly at the rabbit who gazed mildly back, nose twitching. "To be honest, I'm more worried about something getting in than them getting out."

Millie glanced towards the bottom of the plots which, though fenced, backed on to open fields and the country park beyond.

"I've been over everything with a fine-tooth comb; it wouldn't do to let anything happen to them." He looked down at his son and Millie saw sadness in his eyes. She understood why: Cal had suffered enough loss in his short life. Millie had already heard through the allotment grapevine how Nathan's wife had died when Cal was still a toddler.

"Don't worry." Nathan smiled at her, misinterpreting the look in her eyes. "I promise I won't let anything happen to your plot. It's looking extremely splendid, isn't it?"

They both surveyed Millie's allotment for a moment. It lay abundant under the warm sun, a rich patchwork of carefully tended beds divided by neat paths, an opulent profusion of emerald, jade and viridian green.

IT had all come about because the increased bill for Millie's gym membership had arrived the same day she paid two pounds for a small organic lettuce. There was keeping healthy, she'd decided, and there was being insane. Yet unless you counted running up the stairs to her flat and growing a few herbs on the window-sill, there didn't seem to be any alternative.

Until, that was, she passed a mud-encrusted metal gate on her morning run and noticed the neatly tended vegetable beds beyond. It was like switching on a light bulb. An allotment — healthy exercise and lots of lovely organic vegetables, all in one package.

So, one Saturday morning, she became the proud possessor of a neglected, overgrown yet fertile spot in the farthest corner.

Millie had still been a little dubious. Surely allotments were the preserve of elderly men in flat caps, called Alf or Bert?

She soon discovered that while there was both an Alf and a Bert, there was also a Juliet, a Crystal and even a Saskia; not to mention the many others who helped her get started by giving her left over seeds, telling her when to plant shallots and helping her start up the extremely temperamental rotavator.

Two years on, what had once been weed-choked dirt was now a lush garden. Lettuce and beans, peas, courgettes, squash, sturdy young sweetcorn plants and tomatoes; all were thriving. Even the asparagus and artichokes, though still young and not ready to harvest for at least another year, seemed promising.

Millie looked at it all with a sense of deep satisfaction.

"You've done well," Nathan said.

"Oh, it was nothing." Millie smiled. "Just the usual blood, sweat and tears, and hours of back-breaking labour." They grinned at each other.

"Come on then, Cal," Nathan said. "Let's get Barnaby and Britney settled in. Have you brought their food and bedding and everything?"

Father, son and rabbits disappeared into the shed and Millie cheerfully returned to her hoeing.

A S promised, the rabbits were securely housed and let out for their daily hop in a wire-fenced enclosure, carefully supervised by Cal. It was rather pleasant, Millie decided, having Barnaby and Britney next door. Millie got used to arriving at the allotment for evening watering to find Cal and Nathan tending the pets. She started bringing home-made cakes and flapjacks to share with them while she had a short break.

So she wasn't surprised to be met at the allotment gate one evening by Cal. She was concerned, though, that he looked tear-streaked and mutinous.

"I'm sorry, Millie; really, really sorry. I don't think it was them but I'm sorry anyway."

"What is it? What are you sorry about?" Millie was puzzled to see Nathan hurrying towards them, his face creased with anxiety.

"Millie, I'm so sorry . . ."

"You, too? What's everyone so sorry about?"

"Your vegetables . . ." Nathan looked apologetic.

Millie's heart sank. She thought she knew what was coming. She hurried past Nathan then stopped dead as she saw her patch.

It looked as if a madman had attacked it with a lawnmower. Where there had been lush vegetation, there were now raw, bald areas where bare earth showed through. The lettuces had been decimated; the young cabbages were gone. The tops had been ripped off some plants, others left as ragged, leafless stems. Bare stalks grew where three artichoke plants had been; a quarter of the asparagus was gone, as well.

"Oh, no, they can't have . . ." She turned a stricken face to Nathan. "Barnaby and Britney?"

Nathan nodded sadly. He opened his mouth to speak but Cal interrupted him hotly.

"You don't know it was them. It might not have been."

"Cal . . ." Nathan began.

"They were in their cages when I got here. How could it have been them?"

"Cal, what else could it have been?"

Along The Lane

A BULLFINCH sang as I walked along,
Then a sparrow joined in the song.
Out in the fields was a pheasant calling
And a magpie's soft, bright wings were soaring.
Big, fat country pigeons lifted;
In the distance, seagulls drifted.
The hedgerow was full of busy birds,
Happily chattering bright little words.
I saw a rookery up in the trees
And cawing rooks in a morning breeze
Out in the meadow a rabbit sat,
A distance away was the cottage cat.
Dancing blossoms were pale and mild
But over the fields the wind blew wild.
Daffodils nodded beside the farm,
All of nature seemed so calm.
In moments of quiet I'll think again
Of all the wonders along the lane . . .
— Enid Pearson.

"There are rabbits in the field, dozens of them, probably. How do you know it wasn't them?"

Nathan shook his head slowly.

"They've never been a problem, you know that. It can only have been Barnaby and Britney."

"Then why were they in their cages?" Cal yelled.

Nathan sighed, exasperated.

"I don't know; I expect somebody found them and put them back before they could do any more damage."

"And how could they open the shed door without the key?"

"Well . . . If it was already open . . ." Nathan spoke hesitantly, unwilling to accuse his son.

"Because you think I left it open!"

"Cal, calm down."

"I didn't. I know I didn't. I gave them their breakfast as usual and —" Abruptly, he turned and ran back down the path towards the gate.

"Cal! Cal, come back." Nathan turned to Millie, his face full of conflicting emotions. "I'd better go after him. Will you be all right? I don't want to run out on you like this, but . . ."

"No, go. I'll be all right. After all," she said bravely, "it's only a few plants."

"Look, if there's anything you need, take it — lettuce, courgettes, help yourself. I've got some cabbage plants you can have and I'll replace the artichokes and asparagus, of course. We'll do what we can, but all your hard

110

Willie Shand.

work . . ." Nathan gestured helplessly.

Millie thought of her blistered hands, the broken nails, the evenings spent lying in a hot bath to ease her aching back.

"Don't worry. Boys will be boys and, I suppose, rabbits will be rabbits. Go after Cal now, go on."

Alone, she gazed hopelessly at her ravaged plot. How could two rabbits do this much damage? Millie sighed deeply and started to do what she could to repair it.

OVER the next few evenings Millie got her allotment back into something near its original state. Nathan and Cal helped and several people found they had "surplus" plants needing a good home.

But by Saturday morning, Millie arrived at her plot to find another scene of devastation.

"I'll have to take them home," Nathan said worriedly when he saw the damage. "It's too much to expect you to put up with this."

"No, Dad, you can't." Cal was horrified. "What about next-door's cat?"

"Is the new run finished?" Millie asked.

Nathan shook his head.

"I've had to wait for materials."

"It wasn't them, I know it wasn't. Please, Dad . . ." Cal entreated.

Nathan spoke seriously to his son.

"I promise I'll keep them as safe as I can, but we can't leave them here, you must see that. It's not fair on Millie."

"No, really, it's OK . . ." Millie began to protest.

"No," Nathan said firmly.

"Dad . . ."

"It's not the end of the world, honestly," Millie stressed. "It's a few lettuces, that's all. Please let them stay. Besides, suppose something happened to them?"

Nathan looked at Millie, his face heavy with concern.

"I can't let you suffer like this."

"And you can't let Cal suffer, either," Millie said in a low voice. "Let them stay, just for a few more days. After all," she looked around ruefully, "how much more damage can they do?"

Nathan caught her hand impulsively.

"I owe you, Millie. I'll make it up to you, I promise."

"Don't worry." Millie grinned. "I'll have you and Cal digging most of the autumn."

Nathan grinned back, then his face grew sober again.

"I'll come over with Cal at feeding times from now on to make sure they're shut away properly. Thanks for rounding them up and putting them back safely, by the way. Anyone else would have wrung their furry little necks."

Millie frowned.

"But I didn't put them back," she said. "They were in the shed when I arrived."

"See, see," Cal said triumphantly. "It wasn't Barnaby and Britney. I told you it wasn't."

Millie and Nathan looked at each other for a moment, perplexed.

Nathan shrugged.

"Someone must have found them," he said.

"You said that last time, Dad. It wasn't them. It can't have been, can it, Millie?"

"Well, I don't know . . ." Millie said, not wishing to upset Cal further.

"Shush, Cal. That's enough now. We'll have to make absolutely certain it isn't them in the future because if this happens again, they'll have to go home. Understood?"

"But . . ."

"Cal . . ."

"OK, understood."

"Good boy." Nathan ruffled Cal's hair.

*　　*　　*　　*

A few mornings later, Millie woke from a deep sleep. Glancing at her bedside clock, she was surprised to see it was only a quarter to five in the morning. She was just snuggling down again when she heard a series of small, sharp taps. She sat up.

There it was again. Something at the window, like a flurry of hailstones. Hailstones, in June? She got up and peered out at the sky.

"Millie . . ." a soft, urgent voice called.

Millie glanced down and saw Cal standing on the drive, staring up at her. Not hailstones, but gravel. Bemused, she opened the window.

"Cal? Was that you? What are you doing?"

"Millie, please, please come with me. I've got to show you something."

"Come where? It's awfully early, Cal. Can't it wait until later?"

"It can't, honestly it can't. Please, Millie." Cal was practically hopping on one leg with impatience.

Millie noticed a rumpled-looking Nathan coming up the drive behind his son. Seeing her, he shrugged apologetically, as mystified as she was.

She hastily pulled on some clothes and a few minutes later was following Cal and Nathan down the gravel drive, walking gingerly, worried about disturbing the residents of the other flats.

"Cal, where are we going?" Nathan said, yawning.

"You'll see when we get there. You'll see everything when we get there, I promise." Cal smiled at her trustingly.

I must be mad, Millie thought.

Perhaps she wasn't mad, perhaps she was only dreaming. There was definitely something dream-like about the deserted streets filled with bird-song and pearly light. Millie had just decided it must be the shadows going the wrong way that made everything look so strange when Cal stopped outside the gate to the allotments.

"You have to be really, really quiet now," he admonished them.

Millie and Nathan nodded solemnly, even though neither had said a word the whole way there.

CAL opened the gate cautiously, closing it gently behind them. They crept along the path, Cal repeatedly halting while he peered carefully around, then motioning them forward until they reached the shed where the rabbits were. Instead of going inside, though, Cal slipped round the back, beckoning them to follow.

They stood behind the shed for a few minutes, Cal peering intently around the corner.

"Cal, what . . ."

"Shhh." Cal held up a warning finger. "Wait," he breathed.

They waited.

The allotment looked hazy and insubstantial in the early light. Sunshine was just breaking through and the leaves were tipped with pale, shimmering gold. Everything was peaceful and new-looking, as if it had all been made fresh that morning.

This is what Eden must have been like, Millie thought drowsily when she felt Cal's hand on her arm. Excited, he pointed to the fence at the back of Millie's plot.

Something was moving there. Millie and Nathan craned forwards. In the corner where the palings were slightly more widely spaced something squeezed through and stood poised and alert, sniffing the air.

Millie strained her eyes to see. Was it a dog? No, it couldn't be; it was about the right size, but too slight. It picked its way forward gracefully, stepping on slender, delicate legs, then turned to display dark, liquid eyes and a pair of diminutive antlers.

Millie gasped. It was a deer. A tiny deer. She glanced at Cal, who grinned up at her. Two more deer slipped through the gap in the fence. Millie watched, enchanted, even as they started to nibble the tops of her remaining broccoli plants. They were something out of a fairytale.

"Muntjac," Nathan murmured. "Muntjac deer. Well, I never . . ."

Sensing something, the deer's ears pricked and in a flash they were gone.

Cal was exuberant on the way home.

"I told you it wasn't Barnaby or Britney, didn't I? I said, didn't I, and I was right, wasn't I?"

"Yes, all right, Cal," Nathan said for the hundredth time, pulling a wry face at Millie. "I'm never going to be allowed to forget this, you know."

"No, I don't think you are." Millie laughed.

"Something else I'll never forget . . ." Nathan looked awkward. "Well, the way you've handled all of this."

"What, getting up at five in the morning?"

"No, the whole thing. I mean most people would have been . . ."

"Forget it," Millie said, and smiled at him. Nathan smiled back and for a moment Millie was back in Eden.

Cal skipped jubilantly around them.

"I knew it wasn't them so I went up really early yesterday morning and that's when I saw the deer. It must have been them all along, mustn't it, Dad?"

"Yes, Cal, probably it was," Nathan said, his gaze never leaving Millie's face.

*   *   *   *

They contacted the country park and told them their deer were straying and they in turn deer-proofed the fence along the back of the allotment, as well as planting late lettuces in Millie's plot.

Millie held wooden posts and wire netting while Nathan drilled and nailed and finally completed Barnaby and Britney's new run. Next-door's cat, a little less wild after a trip to the vet, looked on lazily as the two rabbits were installed in their new home.

"To Barnaby and Britney." Cal raised a glass of cola and Millie and Nathan raised their own glasses. Barnaby nuzzled contentedly at a pile of chickweed while Britney lolloped around her run, lop ears flopping, injured leg nearly healed.

"They seem happy enough to be home," Millie said.

"So they should, they've got all mod cons there, you know," Nathan said. "I'm surprised Cal hasn't insisted on a Jacuzzi and plasma TV for them."

"Well, you did owe them, I suppose; maligning their reputations like that," Millie teased. "I'm surprised they weren't . . ."

". . . hopping mad?" Nathan grinned at her and Millie swatted at him with her free hand before settling back in her garden chair with the contented feeling that it wasn't only Barnaby and Britney who were coming home. ■

THIS stand-off with the villagers can't go on, ma'am. It's driving the men crazy. I was wondering . . . maybe . . . if you might be able to help."

Friendly exuberance met with thinly veiled suspicion teetering on the edge of hostility. The young American airman from the air-base at nearby Whittingfield stood his ground, twisting his cap in large, capable hands. He was stocky, good-looking, despite his close cropped hair.

"I can't see how," Aunt Edie murmured, who quite clearly didn't, straightening up, her hands full of the crop from the second sowing of peas. They'd done well this year. Ruby, her niece, rested one hand on the handle of her fork and wiped her brow. Digging for victory. The two women had been hard at work all morning, and they were glad of a break.

"I understand you hold some sway with the local

by Susie Riggott.

Illustration by Mark Viney.

A Helping Hand

WVS?" their visitor continued doggedly.

"My, you have been busy." Her aunt's voice was dry. "And you are?"

"Lieutenant Guy Standing, ma'am. Some of the men asked me . . ."

"You mean you've drawn the thin edge of the wedge . . ."

"Not exactly . . ." He was floundering, unsure of what else to say.

Ruby felt sorry for him. Aunt Edie in her sun hat and old gardening clothes was an intimidating spectacle, unless you knew her. But he was right. The villagers should have been more welcoming to their American visitors and something would have to be done.

"Something, anything, ma'am . . . Be much appreciated. The men get upset; they only want to be friendly . . ."

Over friendly and over here? Wasn't that the problem when so many of their hosts had sons and husbands in the thick of the fighting in Europe? These, too, were brave young men and only here to do a job. War was doing odd things to folk, making them behave in a way some would say ought to make them ashamed of themselves.

Aunt Edie took pity, dropping the peas into the basket at her feet, her face softening.

"I'll see what I can do. Leave it with me."

G UY STANDING grinned broadly, a young man who ought to be enjoying life, not stranded miles from home and embroiled in this dreadful war. His gaze slid towards Ruby, and grew warm with something she couldn't mistake.

Cheeks flushing, she resumed her digging, burying her embarrassment in the bundle of potatoes she'd unearthed. Breathing heavily, she hunkered down, sifting her hands through the soil, not looking up when he called goodbye.

"Time for lunch." Aunt Edie threw her an odd look before picking up her basket and leading the way up the path and into the house.

"Are you all right?" she asked quietly, over the omelette they ate at the kitchen table.

The smallholding Aunt Edie had inherited from her parents kept hens, too. With milk from Delilah, the goat, who lived in the meadows at the back of the cottage, they were virtually self-sufficient.

Food was becoming hard to come by, rationing the order of the day. Ever generous, Aunt Edie spread her munificence around, helping many a village family to make ends meet.

Ruby pushed a tomato around her plate, not sure if she wanted to answer. Hard to believe it was over three years since she'd lost Kit. Foolhardy, courageous Kit, returning to rescue one of his men on the beaches of Dunkirk instead of striking out towards the boat waiting to take him to safety.

Coming here to live at Aunt Edie's, throwing herself into the work and the part-time job she'd secured at the coupons office in Derby, had saved her sanity at the time. Of course, she hadn't got over her loss.

She and Kit had had so little married life together, and if only there had been children . . .

She sprang up, took her plate across the kitchen, suppressing a surprising resentment she had no right to feel. Doing what he did was typical of Kit. Would she really have changed him?

"You can't hide away for ever." Aunt Edie's voice was soft and insistent.

"Men are going to look at you, Ruby. You're a good-looking girl. And what harm would there be? You don't imagine Kit . . ."

"Aunt Edie, don't . . ."

She was talking as if Guy Standing had asked her out when he'd only looked. Lots of men looked. And Ruby looked away. She stooped, scraping the contents of her plate into the buckets for scraps, a thing she'd been doing too much of late. She was restless, unsettled. But Kit wouldn't want her to be unhappy.

"I'm not sure I'm ready."

"Of course it's difficult, darling."

She took a deep, calming breath and returned to the table, pouring out tea.

"I've built a new life here, Aunt Edie. I'm happy as it is. You can't tell me you haven't been happy in your single state?"

Aunt Edie was a confirmed spinster, though in her younger days she'd had plenty of offers.

"I suppose I asked for that." Aunt Edie smiled. "That young man had a point, though," she mused, deciding she'd said enough and changing the subject. "Folk don't mean to be unwelcoming, but falling over the American Air Force at every turn has taken some getting used to."

RUBY'S humour was instantly restored. Scornful of the paucity of goods on offer in the village shops, drinking the single pub dry any given day of the week, hands full of candy and chewing gum and stockings, and making eyes at all the girls. No wonder village folk viewed their visitors as creatures from a different planet!

"We need a way of getting everyone together."

"Something like a dance, you mean?"

Aunt Edie shook her head.

"The villagers one side of the room, the Americans another?" She laughed dryly, wise enough to know that would never work. "We need something more intimate. An airman per family, if you see what I mean."

Ruby started to laugh.

"Adopt an airman, you mean?"

"Not that exactly, but . . ." Edie's hand struck the table. "How about an invite to a family meal? Show our visitors a few home comforts, that we're not as bad as they might make out? And they're not as bad as we might think! That would work, I imagine?"

How could it dare not to? Wouldn't folk wish the same for their kith and kin, so far from home, if the rôles were reversed? When Aunt Edie looked so determined, things that needed doing usually got done. Generosity, fairness, hospitality — it didn't need so much effort to point out Mary St Michael's hadn't been quite as welcoming as it might.

Accordingly, after discussions with the local Women's Voluntary Association, of which she was president, a date and list of families willing to provide a good English tea, or as good as could be supplied in these troubled times, was delivered to the base.

I T'S as good a way of getting to know folk as any," Aunt Edie opined, carefully lifting down the best tea service from the dresser. She'd been busy. Boiled

Garden *Glories!*

A TRADITIONAL favourite, but with a twist, is a good way of describing Danse De Feu, a climbing rose. This memorable and vivid climber has strong, upright growth and very dark green foliage. Its double, shapely blooms are a brilliant rich scarlet with a light fragrance that has an almost citrus tang.

This colourful climbing rose flowers all summer to autumn, so you'll be able to enjoy your Danse De Feu for quite a few months. Fully hardy, it prefers a sunny open site, but the good news is that it is definitely a plant that even a complete beginner could cope with!

Photograph courtesy of J. Parker. Telephone 0161 848 1100 for a catalogue or visit www.jparker.co.uk.

eggs, salad, a home-made cake which, if lacking in ingredients, at least looked like a cake.

Where should their names have been other than top of the list? She could hardly expect folk to partake of her scheme if she wasn't prepared to do as much herself. And why shouldn't they entertain a nice family man who would show them pictures of his children and enthral them with stories of life in the States?

When a knock came at the door, even Ruby was surprised at how keen she was to answer it. Life at Windhaven could be lonely; it would do them good to see a fresh face.

"This is wonderfully good of you." The smile of welcome slid away as Guy Standing stepped past her and into the kitchen, taking off his cap to stand, dwarfing the room and looking surprisingly awkward. "We drew lots. Guess I was the lucky one."

"Weren't you just!" Aunt Edie laughed, clearly delighted.

Ruby was blushing again.

Sensing a conspiracy and not understanding how, she kept in the

118

background, busying herself with the tea things and allowing Aunt Edie to play host.

Despite her reservations, as the visit progressed she began to relax. Over tea and after his initial shyness, Guy Standing proved excellent company, needing little prompting to entertain the two women with tales of his life in the States. His father, who ran a garage. His mother, the forceful one, who ran the diner next to the garage where the drivers came in for coffee and passed the time. A family business he hoped to take over some time soon. Hopefully marriage and a family, if he was lucky, even if there was no-one special in his life right now.

Had he meant to look at Ruby quite so directly? His eyes caught hers over the table and held them a fraction too long. Caught out, disconcerted, she looked away too late.

"Why don't you two go for a walk whilst I clear up here?"

Sensing an odd, crackling tension, Aunt Edie stood up and began to stack pots. It would have been churlish to refuse, and what harm was there in walking Guy round the farm? The point of the visit was to make him feel at home and prove the villagers of Mary St Michael's weren't as stand-offish as they appeared.

THE birds were singing evensong. It would be dark soon.

Ruby looked up at her companion, ashamed now that she'd been ungracious. How must he feel so far from home, living amongst strangers and facing the constant dangers of war?

"You must miss the States?" She was awkward and rusty. It had been too long since she'd talked to a young man her age.

For once, Guy's air of American affability slipped, revealing an oddly endearing vulnerability of which she'd never have guessed.

"I tell myself it's still there, waiting," he mused, looking up into the sky at the tiny pin-pricks of stars already appearing and the thin half sliver of moon. It seemed a moment for confidences. He turned towards her, smiling.

"Do you believe in fate? If something happens it's because it was meant?"

Surely what had happened to her life with Kit was never meant? The thought took Ruby's breath, left her bereft of words.

"I feel I was meant to end up here." Guy's gaze bent to hers.

"Are you sure you didn't give it the tiniest hand?"

Guy's eyes lifted, sparkling in a way that told her she wasn't so very wide of the mark.

Ruby led the way round the property, showing him the hens, the gardens, introducing him to Delilah, and unexpectedly telling him about Kit and about her efforts at getting on with her life as she knew he would want.

He was a surprisingly good listener, matching his steps to hers, prompting her when she faltered and found it difficult to put things into words.

"I'm sorry, I had no idea."

"Life goes on." Easy words and all too true. It did and you couldn't stop it. Guy seemed to understand.

"I'll give you a hand in the garden, if you like?" He stood, scratching Delilah behind one ear, looking as if the answer didn't matter when all the while she sensed it did.

"I'm not sure. Aunt Edie . . ."

"Let's ask, shall we?"

Aunt Edie was all for it, as Ruby had known very well, and wouldn't it have been wrong to have spoiled her obvious pleasure in the idea?

AND that was how things went on, summer sliding into autumn, turning Guy into a regular fixture, whenever his flying duties allowed, willingly undertaking the rough digging, cleaning out the hens, learning how to milk Delilah, and making Ruby laugh when she'd not laughed in such a very long time.

Aunt Edie's scheme was proving a resounding success. The Americans were blending into village life in a way surprising to all.

"Out of little acorns?" Guy teased, watching Ruby warmly.

They were sitting by the fire of the only inn the village boasted, drinking a glass of watered-down beer.

"I liked you as soon as I saw you, Ruby," he admitted quietly and then, as if that wasn't enough, taking up her hand and stroking it gently, sending odd, long-forgotten feelings trailing the length of her spine. "Please . . . give us a chance? Ruby, time's so short! Who knows what fate has in store? Surely, you should know that more than anyone?"

"Guy, that's unfair!"

This was war, not fate. She'd been there,

120

been through that. How could she face it all again?

"Guy, it's not that I don't like you, but . . ."

His gaze held hers.

"Ruby . . . I don't want to replace Kit. How could I? Couldn't we just give it a go and see how things turn out?"

It sounded so sensible and that she was the one in the wrong. But if she couldn't cope with her own feelings, how could she cope with his? She shook her head miserably and stood up.

"I don't want this, Guy. There isn't an us."

"How do you know if you won't even try?"

"I don't want to try!" Not daring to examine her spinning emotions, aware that to stay would be more than she could handle, she grabbed her bag from the table and hurried out.

THE following day was her day at the office. She cycled into Derby, burying herself in work, only relieved when it was over and she could go home to an evening avoiding the unspoken curiosity in Aunt Edie's eyes.

She was unsettled and glad to get out on the farm, to the warmth of Delilah's nose bumping gently at her calves, demanding supper. She tipped the contents of the pail into the trough, straightening up and gazing upwards at the night which was a dark one, the moon obscured by a thick blanket of cloud. A good night for flying, Guy once said, because clouds concealed so much.

The ominous drone of bombers from the aerodrome grew louder, dark shapes overhead. How did she know he was up there, exposed and vulnerable, at the whim of uncaring fate? Her own stomach twisting in sympathy, she finished up and trailed inside.

"Something's up," she muttered, her hands curling round the mug Aunt Edie pushed towards her.

"Brave men, in case we're in danger of forgetting."

Was there a hint of accusation in her voice? She wasn't normally so reticent. If anything wanted saying, Aunt Edie usually said it, but some things were better left unsaid. Ruby finished her milk, glad to escape to bed.

There was no escape. Thoughts, pressing and unpalatable, raced round her head, chasing her. Finally, hours later, sleepless and exhausted, she got up from her tangled sheets to stand watching the first rays of dawn chasing shadows over the hills she'd grown to love.

Strands of pale rose warmed her face, filling the room with a golden light, and a thought which took lodging, refusing to budge.

Hastily, trembling, though not from cold, she pulled open the drawer to the dressing table and took out the case holding Kit's service medals. Brave Kit. And brave Guy, too! Didn't both men deserve better?

Aunt Edie was still asleep. Quickly, quietly, not wishing to waken her, she threw on some clothes and hurried downstairs.

Outside, ignoring Delilah's plaintive good mornings, she retrieved her bike from the lean-to and cycled into the village and down towards the aerodrome.

I NEED to see Lieutenant Guy Standing!" She sounded urgent. How ridiculously intent, the words bursting out even before she'd slid to a halt and dismounted.

"That may not be possible, ma'am." The guard was impassive, middle-aged, his face giving nothing away.

"A message, then?"

"That may not be possible either, ma'am."

Something in his voice slid shivers down Ruby's back. She stared, eyes widening. Fate wouldn't, couldn't be so cruel? Her mind refused to accept the thought and thrust it away as the man's face cracked, split with an emotion he could no longer conceal.

"I'm sorry, lady. The squadron's back, missing a plane. I guess . . . Hang in there, ma'am, we can only pray . . ."

Hadn't she prayed so hard before? Her lips were moving, all the same. At that moment, far away in the distance, a speck appeared, a blot against the sky-line. The tiny, angry humming of bees headed their way and grew miraculously louder and larger. Large and angry enough to catch her attention and reveal itself for what it was.

"A plane!" she breathed. A shout of pure joy burst from her, telling her so much — as if she hadn't worked it out already.

The unmistakable sight of a B17 Flying Fortress, wings burnished in sunlight and losing height at an alarming pace, limped toward the airfield.

The engine spluttered and the machine dipped alarmingly before skimming the top of the perimeter fence by the narrowest of margins and hitting the runway, eventually slithering to a clumsy halt.

"Oh, my word!" she cried, her bike crashing to the ground, her feet flying, following the men bursting from the huts and converging towards the stricken vessel which, defying all odds and the wrecked compass that sent it spinning so wildly off course, had landed so miraculously intact.

The door burst open, the crew already jumping down and whooping in happiness to be home unhurt, and shaking the hands of the men running towards them. One, stockier than the others, was standing resting one hand against the fuselage, breathing deeply as if he couldn't believe he was safe.

"Guy?" She slid to a halt several feet in front of him.

Living was for now, for doing what Kit would have wanted and reclaiming her life.

"The other night . . . I'm sorry . . . I'd love us to . . ."

Her sentence remained unfinished, buried in Guy's flying jacket as, with a cry of happiness, he stepped towards her and folded her into his arms. ■

Shopping Around

by Christine Evans.

'D noticed over the weeks that I was working in my sister Amber's boutique that we girls can be broadly divided into two different types. There are those who just adore shoes and handbags — and those who don't.

Personally, I'm not a handbag person. I usually shove my keys and purse into my pockets — plus a lippy, if I remember. My sister, on the other hand, could stand and drool over a new batch of handbags for ages as she arranged them to their best advantage.

"Look at this, Clemmie — isn't it adorable?" she'd ask, showing yet another bag with attachments and buckles that just seemed superfluous to me. "It's the latest."

"It looks just like that other one to me," I confessed. "Except in a different colour."

"Oh, Clem," she'd say, shaking her head in despair.

I usually go around in jeans and T-shirts — most of them bought from the charity shop,

Illustration by Sailesh Thakrar.

123

too, to help eke out my student loan — but Amber insisted that I dressed in the boutique's clothes while I was working there. I was studying marketing and commerce at college and helped her out at weekends and holidays for some extra cash.

But there was no way I could walk about in killer heels all day, as she did. I usually wore ballet pumps for comfort.

Amber seemed to be making a success of her business. Hers was the only shop of its kind in our small town, so her goods were in demand. She knew her stuff, too, and her advice about outfits was always spot on! She always had a small selection of shoes and boots on display with the promise that she could order a customer's choice to arrive within a few days.

Basically, I just did what she told me, fetching and carrying from the stock room and things like that.

Having such different tastes, it was surprising that we both fancied the same sort of man — well, the same man, really.

HE called in one Friday morning looking harassed. It was during my holidays, so I was working in the shop more or less full time. He hung about by the door, glancing furtively at the handbags.

"Can I help you?" I asked.

"I need a bag for my girlfriend," he said. "It's her birthday. We passed your shop the other day and there was this bag in the window. She said it was called a 'decibel' — or something like that." His voice trailed away helplessly.

Amber beamed.

"Oh, you mean the 'Decima'. I know which one you mean. Ours aren't the genuine article, of course — much too expensive — but it's a design that looks closest to it. There are subtle differences, but ours are very good quality — silk lining."

"Well, can I have one?" our customer asked, looking anxious to escape. He obviously wasn't comfortable in the world of women's fashion.

"I'm afraid the one in the window has been sold, as you can see," Amber said, "but we have it in ivory with navy trim."

He nodded.

"OK. Er . . . can I bring it back if it's not right?"

"Certainly, sir," Amber said, still smiling as she turned to me.

"Clemmie, can you get the bag from the stock room?"

I looked blank.

"What's it like?"

Shaking her head in despair, she went to find it herself.

"I'm not hot on bags," I confessed to the customer.

He grinned.

"Me, neither! But Lois seemed keen on this decibel thing."

We chatted while we waited for my sister to return. He was nice straightforward and not bad-looking — although, of course, he belonged to someone else; just my luck, I thought. Sometimes you just click with someone and you feel as if you've known them for ages.

He told me he worked at the town hall, in planning. I mentioned I'd like to work there in tourism and publicity when I finished college. I was just about to find out his name when Amber returned, clutching the bag.

"I knew I had it somewhere," she said triumphantly. "Clemmie, will you wrap it?"

Now if there's one thing I'm good at, it's gift wrapping. Amber asked subtle questions as I worked. Then I presented the package to him with curls of ribbon and a pretty card matching the paper.

"She'll be pleased with that," Amber and I chorused.

"Let's hope so," he said with a grin. "Thanks very much."

We preened, we smiled, we waved as he left.

"He was nice," I said.

"He certainly was," Amber said, with a sigh. "Fancy a man making an effort about a handbag. Lucky girl."

B UT obviously the girl in question didn't feel lucky. The same man called in on Monday evening just before the shop shut. My beautiful gift wrapping was in tatters as he extricated the bag from a plastic one and held it out to Amber.

"It seems she was expecting the genuine article," he said flatly.

"Oh!" we both said together, in surprise. The price of the genuine bags was exorbitant.

"She called me a mean . . ." He stopped abruptly. "Well . . . never mind. Could I have a refund?"

Amber hesitated.

"I'm sorry . . . It's just that you aren't entitled unless . . . But I can give you a credit note," she added eagerly.

"That'll have to do, then," he said wearily. "I don't think my mother would have any use for such a fancy bag. And my sister — well, she always thought Lois was a bit over the top, anyway."

Personally, I agreed with his sister, but of course I didn't say anything.

"And your name is?" Amber prompted, smiling seductively as she wrote out a credit note.

"Hugh Peters," he said.

She didn't strictly need to know his name, but I couldn't blame her for asking.

I smiled sympathetically as he left, but, of course, he didn't look back.

"You could have given him a refund," I protested to Amber.

She grinned.

"But he wouldn't have come back then, would he — our Hugh Peters?"

125

"He'll probably give the credit note to his mum or his sister, anyway," I said. I felt disappointed that we probably wouldn't see him again.

✳   ✳   ✳   ✳

I usually make sandwiches for lunch, but a few mornings later, I overslept and had to leave the house in a bit of a rush.

Amber rarely makes her own lunch, and the fridge in her flat upstairs was empty, as usual, so at lunchtime I went out to buy something for us both.

I was in the queue at the baker's when "our Hugh Peters" came in.

I did a double-take and then decided instantly not to waste any time.

"Oh, hi," I said warmly.

He stared at me and then grinned.

"Of course — the bag lady . . . I mean . . ."

"I know what you mean," I said, with a chuckle.

I lingered with my bag of sandwiches and we left the shop together.

"You haven't been in to see us with your credit note yet," I remarked, simply for the sake of something to say.

"My sister's wedding's coming up," he told me. "I think my mum might call in to see if you have anything special."

"I'm sure we'll find something for her," I said.

"Yes, I told her you were helpful," he said, smiling. "Anyway, I'll mention it again. Clemmie, isn't it?"

You can't imagine the thrill I felt that he'd remembered my name.

"I was reading a book about Churchill around the time I first came into your shop — that was his wife's name," he explained.

Then he left me with a friendly wave.

I'VE just seen 'our Hugh Peters'," I told Amber.

"Hmm," she said thoughtfully. "I saw you from the window. I seemed to remember he was better dressed than that."

She went back to checking her stock without further comment and I was left to daydream about him. It was a bit useless, really, as he hadn't seemed to be particularly interested in me. But a girl can dream, can't she?

I purposely forgot my sandwiches again next day in the hope that I might spot him at the baker's. But Amber had other ideas.

"I'm popping to Giancarlo's for a ciabatta," she said with an enigmatic smile. "Would you like me to get you anything for lunch?"

Giancarlo's was the newly opened Italian pizzeria next door. They served evening meals and did brisk business in pizzas and lunchtime snacks to take away.

Amber had worried at first that the lovely aromas circulating in our stock room would taint the clothes. But then Giancarlo himself had arrived with a complimentary pizza.

126

The River Tay, Perthshire, Scotland

*O*N a drive from Carlisle to Aberdeen, the part of the journey that I look forward to the most is the view of the silvery Tay from the motorway. Depending on the weather, this lovely river can be sky blue or deep, dark grey, but it is always worth a second look and can make a long journey pass that bit quicker.

My daughter, who lives up in Aberdeen, is just about to have her first baby, so no doubt my husband and I will be seeing lots more of the River Tay over the next few months. I just hope the weather will be as good as it was in your artist's picture!

— *Mrs B.J., Carlisle.*

J. CAMPBELL KERR.

"For-a my lovely neighbours," he'd announced.

What a charming accent — and what a smoothie, I thought!

Amber was impressed, though.

"His brother imports Italian shoes and handbags," she said with that same smile. "He's setting up a meeting for us one evening. Hopefully, we'll be able to do some business."

I had to admit his Parma ham and mozzarella ciabattas were to die for — but expensive.

I made my own sandwiches next day and just hung around longingly in the window at lunchtime for a glimpse of Hugh. The moment I noticed him going into the baker's, I rushed to get my purse. But he was on the way out again by the time I'd reached our shop door. For a moment, I thought he glanced over in the direction of our shop, but I couldn't be sure.

A FEW days later, his mum and sister arrived at the shop clutching the credit note. They were both really nice.

"My son did say you were lovely girls," his mum said, looking delighted as I showed her a lilac dress with matching jacket.

I warmed to her immediately.

"That's gorgeous, Mum," the bride-to-be said. "It'll be perfect for you. Now we just need to find a hat."

We tried fascinators, we tried floppy hats, wide-brimmed hats and fussy hats, but the one that suited her best was a small one in the same shade as the dress.

Even I could tell that it was the perfect hat for her.

"That's the one," I said and the others agreed with me.

Mrs Peters glimpsed at the price ticket and bit her lip.

"It's a bit more than I wanted to pay," she admitted shyly. "I mean, I'm not likely to wear it again . . . "

"Oh, go on, Mum — treat yourself!" her daughter urged.

"I'll think about it," she said cautiously.

I knew how she felt. My mum would have had the same misgivings about spending so much.

It was very expensive. A designer friend of Amber's makes her hats for her and she has to make a profit.

As I said goodbye to the Peters family, I felt sad. They were nice people — and the son was nice, too.

"Pity she couldn't be persuaded," Amber remarked. "I had those sandals with the crystals on the straps just ready to offer her — and the little matching clutch bag."

"The heels would have been too high for her," I argued, thinking of our own mum and what she would feel comfortable in.

"I suppose so," Amber admitted grudgingly.

It was just before closing on Saturday evening a week later when Amber called me through from the stock room, saying she needed some help in the shop.

When I went through, though, there was only one person there. But she gave me a wink.

"It's our Hugh Peters," she mouthed.

"There's this hat . . ." he began, looking embarrassed.

"The one your mum looked lovely in," I said with a huge smile.

"That's right," he said, looking relieved.

"My sister said I should come in and buy it as a surprise. They've looked everywhere and not found anything suitable. It's Mum's birthday next month so we've decided to buy the hat between us."

"Oh, she'll love it," I said warmly. "It really does suit her and goes beautifully with her outfit."

Amber arrived with a hat box.

"Knock a tenner off the price, Clemmie," she said with a smile, placing the hat carefully into the box with tissue-paper.

He looked delighted.

"Thanks a million. I'm so glad you remembered. I'm really grateful," he said.

I smiled winningly at him as I added a fancy bow to the box.

H E picked up the box and sort of hovered, although Amber tactlessly brought out the vacuum cleaner.

"I . . . erm . . . I haven't seen you in the baker's recently," he commented.

"No, I've been bringing my own sandwiches to save money," I explained.

"Of course — you're a student. I was thinking about you when I called in on our tourist information office the other day."

Amber switched on the noisy cleaner just then and he began backing towards the door.

"I . . . er . . . I suppose I'd better be going."

"Please call again," I said — a bit too pathetically — as I opened the door for him. "If ever you need any . . ."

"Hats or handbags!" he said, laughing. "I wouldn't go anywhere else. You've been brilliant."

I gazed at his back as he walked down the high street and was rewarded as he turned and smiled.

"You could have waited with the flipping vac." I rounded on Amber angrily. "You rushed him out."

"I'm going to Giancarlo's this evening," she said with a smirk. "I need time to pamper myself before I go."

"Pamper yourself? What on earth for? You're only going to order some old shoes and bags!" I retorted.

She sighed.

"You don't get it, do you?" she said, shaking her head in despair. "It's not just the shoes and the bags — it's . . . well, it's Giancarlo."

"Oh!"

I felt very silly that I hadn't noticed.

"You've been too busy mooning over Hugh Peters to notice," she said with a grin. "Don't think I haven't seen you gawping out of the window at lunchtime."

I didn't think I'd been that obvious.

"When I called you into the shop, I thought you might have given him a bit more encouragement," she said. "But 'Please call again'? For goodness' sake, Clemmie, it's not very . . . well, you know . . ."

She was right — I'm hopeless at flirting.

"Never mind," she added with a curious smile. "He might find a little surprise in with the hat."

"What do you mean?" I demanded.

She just winked at me.

"You'll see — I hope. I'd better be going — see you at Sunday lunch tomorrow."

So I was left none the wiser.

She arrived, looking radiant, at our house the next day. Apparently she'd made a great deal over shoes and handbags with Giancarlo's brother — and when he'd left, she and Giancarlo had lingered over the coffee.

"We're going to an Italian opera next Thursday," she said with the smile of a satisfied cat.

Lucky her.

I FOUND out what she'd been up to with the hat, though. Hugh came shyly into the shop at Monday lunchtime. He hovered, looking very embarrassed, until the last customer had left.

"Can I help you?" I asked with a beaming smile.

"Sort of . . . I mean, I hope so. I was wondering . . . My sister found this 'two for one voucher' from the restaurant next door in the hat box."

So that's what Amber had been up to!

"I was wondering . . ." he continued. "I mean, it isn't just because it's an offer . . . It just seems a good opportunity . . . that is, if you'd like . . ."

Would I like? If only he knew.

Amber may well have been successful in her attempt to play Cupid, but she couldn't persuade me to wear high heels on my date.

Which is just as well, really, because "my Hugh Peters" has had enough of high-maintenance girlfriends.

"The thing I first liked about you, Clemmie, was that you look so pretty without all the paraphernalia and make-up," he said, seconds after kissing me tenderly.

He tasted of garlic. I expect I did, too. Who would have expected garlic to taste so sweet? ■

130

The Minstrel

DRIFTING through the morning air, melodious and sweet,
Above the crowds and traffic of a very busy street,

Refreshing as the summer rain, as light as any cloud,
The music casts its magic on the people all around.

For just a fleeting moment, we are spellbound with her song,
And all is just forgotten as she carries us along.

A voice as soft as thistledown, she plucks her old guitar,
Our spirits soar with smiles galore, just standing where we are.

And when her song is over, with our business to resume,
We find our day is brightened by the minstrel's lovely tune.

— *Sandra Robinson.*

131

IT had been a brilliant day. The pockets of our makeshift costumes were bulging with sweets and between the three of us we'd scoffed enough apples to stock the greengrocer's for a week.

Our hollowed-out turnip lanterns glowed steadily as we made our way down the darkening lane, feet shuffling through brown leaves that, just the week before, had been as bright as newly minted pennies on the overhead branches.

I'd always loved the crunch of walking on fallen leaves, and was glad we hadn't listened to Wendy. She'd said we should do things differently this year, and go guising on our bikes. But she only wanted to show off the new Chopper she'd been given for her birthday earlier that month. I soon put a stop to that idea, even though she was my best friend. I mean, it's hardly a broomstick, is it?

We reached the end of the lane and turned into the last street we planned to visit before home: Sutton Avenue.

Everything had been fine until then. We'd been discussing which sweets to share first when we got home: my rhubarb and custard chews or Wendy's pineapple chunks.

Then I realised that my sister Josie hadn't put in a word for her favourite peanut brittle. In fact, she'd been silent for some minutes. Her pace had slowed to a crawl, as well, and she was dragging Mum's yard broom along instead of carrying it.

"Come on, Josie!" I called over my shoulder. "The clocks went back last night, remember? It'll be dark soon. Get a move on!"

A tug on the edge of my ragged cloak told me she'd caught up.

"Can we go home now?"

I guessed she was tired. She was only eight years old, and we'd been out for quite a while.

"Just one more to go," I said, pointing down the road. "Number twenty-three . . ."

"No! Not twenty-three!"

*Illustration by
Patricia Ludlow.*

"But it's only the Baileys," Wendy said. "What's wrong with them, all of a sudden?"

What, indeed? True, the house was set back a bit from the

132

pavement, with a tall poplar in the front that, when dusk fell, cast a shadow like an ogre's on to the neat lawn. But the lights shining from the curtained windows were friendly, as were the retired couple within.

We often visited them on the way home from school. Mr Bailey gave us strawberries from his allotment in summer, and Mrs Bailey usually slipped us a home-made biscuit or two before we left. And we always, always visited them on Hallowe'en.

But, now I thought of it, Josie hadn't been near them for ages. That was especially odd because they'd recently taken in a stray cat, and she adored animals. I held my lantern up to her face and was shocked by how pale she looked, even through the sooty smears on her cheeks.

"What's the matter?" I asked her. "Hallowe'en is meant to be fun! You're not scared, are you?"

Josie shook her head fiercely, but continued to hang back.

"Well, don't be silly, then," I said, aware that Wendy was becoming impatient. "Besides, this is the quickest way home. The only other way is past Old Knobbly, and that really would scare you!"

THAT'LL bring her to her senses, I thought. The withered old oak tree on the common, with its fire-blackened hollow gaping like a toothless mouth, was the subject of many playground legends, and most of us avoided that route after sunset.

Josie whimpered, but refused to move, and I saw with alarm that her grey eyes were brimming with tears.

by Nina Curle.

133

"Josie! Whatever's wrong?"

"Don't make me go there, Anna!" she blurted out. Her voice dropped to a frightened whisper. "Mrs Bailey is a — a murderer!"

WE stared at her in astonished silence while this sank in.

"You can't go around saying things like that!" I cried. "Mum'll be hopping mad if she hears you're making up wicked stories about the neighbours."

"But I'm not!" She sobbed. "And I've never told anyone till now. Please don't go in there — she might kill you, too!"

Thrown by this unexpected turn of events, I tried to think sensibly.

I knew Josie wasn't given to telling lies, but she did have a lurid imagination and sometimes got things wrong. She'd been adamant one summer that fairies were living around the school pond, and it took for ever to convince her that the gossamer-winged creatures she'd seen were dragonflies. So the first thing to do was find out if this was a similar mistake.

"OK." I faced Josie. "What makes you think Mrs Bailey is a murderer?"

"It was when I was collecting jumble for the Brownies." She gave a gulp. "Mr Bailey was cutting the grass and told me to go on in. So I went into the hall . . . and that's when I saw Mrs Bailey come through, with — with blood all over her hands!

"She was wiping them on a cloth — and it was all bloodstained, too, and she said, 'Oh, it's you, Josie. Excuse me while I get rid of the evidence.' Then she went to wash the blood off!"

"But who did she kill?" Wendy asked, wide-eyed.

"I don't know. I ran away before she could get me, too!"

No amount of quizzing would make her change her story. It was growing darker by the minute, and a chill breeze sprang up, making me shiver.

Being the eldest by three years and one month, it was down to me to make a decision. Wendy and I had been studying Shakespeare at school and thoughts of Lady Macbeth came uncomfortably to mind. But I'd never seen anything worse than flour on Mrs Bailey's hands. There had to be an innocent explanation.

I knew what the gang from our favourite cartoon, "Scooby-Doo", would do: go and look for clues to unravel the mystery! Maybe we should, too . . .

"We can't stand here all evening," I said, "and if we don't go, they'll think something's wrong. So we'll go, but stick close together, and keep an eye out for anything suspicious."

Josie gave a whine, and even Wendy shifted her feet uncertainly. I wasn't feeling too comfortable, either, but tried to swallow my doubts.

"It's all very strange," I remarked, taking Josie's hand and remembering to use the Green Cross Code before we crossed the street. "They both go to our church and Mrs Bailey bakes for the WRI. Still, she can't kill all three of us, not without someone noticing."

"If anyone knows where we've gone . . ." Wendy murmured darkly.

THE Baileys welcomed us as they had every previous Hallowe'en, and we filed into the kitchen, where we went through our usual selection of songs and poems. Everything seemed quite normal, with no hint of anything odd so far, although Josie was still pale and shaky.

"And how are you, Josie, dear?" Mrs Bailey asked when we'd taken a bow. "We've not seen you since August, when you came round for the jumble. And you'd gone by the time I'd hunted something out for you."

"Er . . . she was feeling unwell that day," I said quickly, seeing Josie's lower lip start to tremble.

Mrs Bailey smiled and turned towards the tray on the table.

"I've got a special treat for you tonight," she announced. "One of your favourite cakes, baked fresh this afternoon . . . plus an extra surprise! Just go through to the front room and Mr Bailey will . . ."

Whatever she'd been about to say was lost in the wail from Josie. She sank to her knees and started to howl.

The noise brought Mr Bailey rushing back into the kitchen. Mrs Bailey stood with her mouth open.

"Whatever is it?" he cried. "I thought the banshees had paid us a visit!"

I knelt down beside Josie and put my arm around her. Wendy looked on, ashen-faced.

"She's just a bit tired." I didn't know what else to say. This dear old couple seemed perfectly harmless, and yet my sister was scared stiff!

Suddenly Josie stood up, tears running in sooty streaks down her face.

"Don't let them make me eat anything." She sobbed. "It might be poisoned!"

Horrified, I looked over at our hosts. They both wore blank expressions.

Then Mr Bailey sat down in the nearest chair, his face level with Josie's.

"You'd better explain yourself, young lady," he said.

Silence descended after Josie had stumbled through her awful tale. We waited uneasily to see what would happen next.

For a moment Mrs Bailey stared ahead, as if trying to recall the events of that fateful day. Then, suddenly, she threw her head back and laughed.

It wasn't the evil cackle of an unmasked villain, but more like a fit of the giggles. The four of us, Mr Bailey included, watched in astonishment as tears of laughter streamed down the crinkles in her cheeks.

"Just a moment!" she spluttered, and left the room.

Hardly daring to breathe, we stared at each other. This was turning into the strangest Hallowe'en ever!

Mrs Bailey returned, carrying a small jar.

"Was this what you saw?" she asked, opening the jar and plunging a fork inside.

We gasped at the vivid stain on the fork, and at the object on its prongs.

"Josie!" I cried. "You idiot! It's beetroot juice!"

My sister's jaw dropped as she gazed at the bright liquid dripping on to the beige Formica table.

"Josie's right," Mr Bailey said, dipping his finger into the puddle of juice and holding it up to the light. "It does look a bit like blood, doesn't it? But then," he gave a chuckle, "things are not always what they seem in life!"

"But Mrs Bailey." I frowned. "Why did you say you had to get rid of the evidence, when you were just pickling beetroot?"

Mrs Bailey laughed again.

"That's just my way of speaking. I meant I needed to make myself presentable before company. I'd say the same if you caught me up to my elbows in soap suds."

"Oh, Mrs Bailey," Josie said, throwing her arms around her, "I'm so glad you're not a murderer after all!"

"So am I, dear." She smiled. "Otherwise you wouldn't be able to come and visit any more. Or see our special surprise . . ."

LATER, sitting cosily by the fire, we made friends with the Baileys' stray cat — and her three kittens.

"We had no idea she was expecting when we took her in," Mr Bailey explained. "The kittens will soon be old enough to leave home and — if your parents agree — you can each have one."

"They'll agree!" we chorused.

Mr Bailey was right: things are not always as they seem — especially at Hallowe'en! We had arrived full of apprehension, and were leaving with Josie's faith in Mrs Bailey restored and the prospect of a new kitten each in November.

It really had been a brilliant day! ■

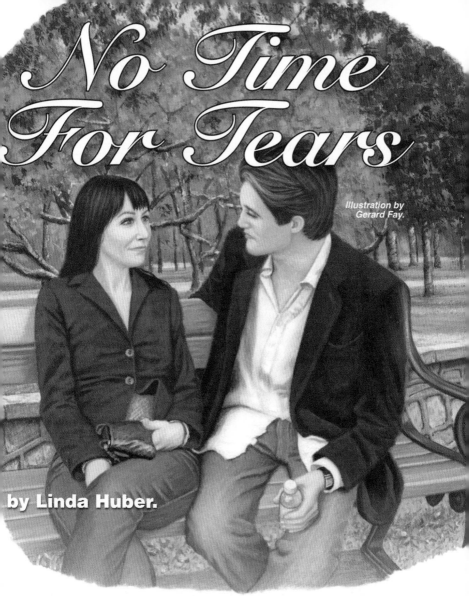

No Time For Tears

Illustration by Gerard Fay.

by Linda Huber.

R OB MCLELLAN squeezed his long frame into the window-seat and pushed his rucksack under the seat in front. The last few passengers were boarding, and the flight attendants were busy helping people stow their hand luggage and banging the overhead lockers firmly shut.

The plane wasn't full, Rob realised, craning his neck and looking round. In fact, he had a whole row of three seats to himself. So it would be a nice, peaceful flight, and he'd have plenty of time to think about how best to help

Dad with the removal.

"Ladies and gentlemen, this is Ron Taylor, your captain, speaking. Welcome to this morning's flight from London Heathrow up to Edinburgh. We're just waiting for the last remaining passenger to board and then we'll be off. Our flight time today will be . . ."

Rob stopped listening. He'd flown this stretch so many times before that there wasn't much he didn't already know about flight times and altitudes. He'd been back to Edinburgh every couple of months, at least, ever since he'd started his job in London five years ago.

London was home now — he had his own flat, his job, loads of friends, even a cat. He was well and truly settled in the south. But Edinburgh — that was . . . special. Maybe all the more since he'd lost his mum there when he was just fourteen. His treasured memories of her were stronger on the streets of his home town.

There was a short disturbance at the front of the plane as the "last remaining passenger", a young woman with long dark hair and a pale face, boarded. To Rob's slight dismay, the flight attendant showed the girl to the aisle seat on his row. He smiled politely as she sat down and fastened her safety belt. Hopefully she wouldn't want to talk all the time — he needed some space to think.

THE plane taxied to the runway, and took off with the usual stomach-lurching swoosh. Rob closed his eyes. This would be the last time he'd fly from Heathrow to Edinburgh to visit Dad. Next time, he'd be flying to Glasgow. His father had recently seized the opportunity to buy a little flat in the same building as his sister, Enid.

"I'm not getting any younger, son, and neither are Enid and Bob. Only sensible to stick together in our old age," he'd joked.

Rob had been completely taken aback. Dad had moved to Edinburgh when he and Mum had married, over forty years ago now. It would be an enormous upheaval to leave the place after all that time.

OK, they didn't have any close relatives nearby, apart from a family of second cousins in North Berwick, but still . . . Dad had all his friends, his darts club and the book club, and the birdwatchers' society — all in Edinburgh. Not to mention the garden, and his voluntary work in the thrift shop.

Rob became aware that the young woman beside him was mopping her eyes with a tissue. By the look of things, she wasn't having an easy time, either. Rob hesitated, then decided to speak. After all, she could only bite his head off once.

"Are you OK? Can I do anything?" he asked. To his relief, she gave him a watery grin.

"Thanks, I'm fine, really. It's just that I haven't had time to sit down and drink since it happened, and it's suddenly all sort of hit me."

Rob nodded, unsure how to reply to this. An introduction seemed the best way.

"I'm Rob McLellan. Going home to Edinburgh to help my dad move to Glasgow."

The girl shook hands.

"Katie Lennox. I'm going to my sister's home in Edinburgh to look after her three kids while she and her husband stay with the new baby in the children's hospital."

"Oh, dear — I hope it's nothing serious."

"Not very, but she was born late last night, four weeks early. She'll need a little operation to remove a cyst in her mouth. The doctors say she'll be fine, but it was still a shock. You don't expect things like that to happen. Fortunately, I'm due some time off work, so that wasn't a problem."

The relief on her face was apparent, and Rob thought about his own family. He had no brothers or sisters to supply nephews and nieces to babysit. And up until now, he'd never really considered this as something lacking in his life.

But then, a family with children — wasn't that what most people wanted at some point in their lives? Look at Katie, with her big extended family — they were obviously very important to her.

Oh, dear. He didn't really want to think about the pros and cons of big families right now. Dad's removal was enough to worry about at the moment.

＊　　＊　　＊　　＊

As if in sympathy with Rob's gloomy mood, it was raining when they touched down in Edinburgh. Katie, who had been silent for most of the trip, turned to him with a rueful grin.

"That was probably the last peaceful hour I'll have at this time of day for a while," she said.

"Families, eh?" Rob said, noticing that she was looking much brighter now. The thought of seeing her sister and the children was obviously a very pleasant one.

"Um, I'm going to hire a car," he said carefully. "Can I drop you off anywhere?"

She shook her head.

"Thanks, but my brother-in-law's picking me up and we're going straight to the hospital," she said. "Oh, gosh, I can't wait!"

As soon as the plane reached the terminal she was on her feet.

"Good luck with the removal," she said, edging into the aisle.

"Thanks. I hope everything goes well for your family," Rob said, watching as she squeezed her way towards the door.

He saw her again in the terminal building, a toddler in her arms and two

139

small boys jumping around beside her. The man talking to her must have bee[n] the brother-in-law. They all disappeared towards the car park.

And now it was time to think of his own family — Dad.

HALF an hour later, Rob was pulling up outside the house that ha[d] been his childhood home. A good-sized semi, ivy growing up th[e] front, a neat garden front and back. A lump came into his throat. Po[or] Dad — he must be feeling awful at the thought of leaving all of this.

His father's face, however, was one big, beaming smile when he opened th[e] front door.

"Hello, son! You made good time. Come and have a coffee and get settle[d] and I'll show you all the old stuff I found in the attic. There's a lot mo[re] besides."

Three steps into the house showed Rob that his old home no longer existe[d]. The hallway was filled with boxes, packed and waiting to go. All the litt[le] knick-knacks, like the Capo di Monte rose that used to be on the window-si[ll] and all the pictures, were gone.

Phil McLellan clapped his son's shoulder.

"I've made a good start, as you can see," he said. "But I'm glad you're he[re] to lend a hand with the heavier stuff. Come on, coffee's in the kitchen."

Later that evening, having spent several hours organising the contents [of] the attic, as well as the few things of his own that were still there, Rob lay i[n] bed and let the memories flood over him.

An Edinburgh childhood: primary school, Scouts, secondary school (an[d] all that homework). Then he'd left to do a business degree in Glasgo[w] travelling to Edinburgh almost every weekend — and then London.

Soon, now, there wouldn't be a home in Edinburgh to come back to, an[d] for some reason, Dad almost seemed happy about it.

Rob tossed and turned for most of the night and then got up early to make [a] much-needed cup of coffee. Phil came in while he was drinking it.

"Ready for action?" he asked, spreading honey lavishly on a piece of toas[t]. "If you box up all the books still in the bookcase, ready to go to the thri[ft] shop, I'll wrap up the ornaments I want to take with me. You can see if there[']s anything you want, too, and the rest of it can go to the shop. I'm not takin[g] the display cabinet — there's no room for it in my new wee flat."

Rob armed himself with a duster and started on the books. Most of the[m] had been his mother's — she'd been a great reader. He smiled, rememberin[g] how she'd always insisted on taking at least three books on holiday with he[r] and then a huge lump came into his throat. Most of Mum's books an[d] ornaments were going to end up in the thrift shop. Was that really what [he] wanted — what she'd have wanted?

Phil came in while he was still blinking dismally into a well-read copy [of] "Black Beauty".

140

Melton Mowbray, Leicestershire, England

I WAS delighted to see your beautiful painting of Melton Mowbray. Living in nearby Nottingham, my husband and I were reminded of the fabulous Melton Mowbray markets that we used to visit when we fancied a day out. We still frequent the car boot sales on a Sunday, and have picked up more than our fair share of bargains! I'd recommend a trip to the markets to anyone. There's always a lot going on.

Of course, before we ever left the town, my husband would insist on picking up an old-fashioned pork pie or two from Dickinson & Morris! Happy memories indeed!

— Mrs K.C., Nottingham.

CAMPBELL KERR

"Cheer up, son," he said. "They're only books, and no-one's read any of them for years."

"They were Mum's books," Rob mumbled, and Phil patted his shoulder.

"Aye, and she'd have been the first to want them to go to a good home," he said firmly. "And she wouldn't want you to be standing there with your face tripping you because of her books, either. I'm not getting rid of anything important, Rob. The photos are all packed up safely — and the memories," he said, tapping his head with his finger.

Rob nodded slowly. He was being too emotional, he could see that now.

"But don't you regret leaving your home? And your friends?" he burst out before he could stop himself.

Phil actually laughed.

"This is just a house, son. And it's too big for me, you know. The memories are all safe in my head. My friends here'll be just a short train ride away. Anyway, Glasgow is home — it's where I grew up."

*   *   *   *

Rob finished packing the books and loaded the boxes into the car. He would take them to the thrift shop, and then collect some more removal boxes from that place behind Princes Street. He wanted to have a think about what Dad had said, too.

The thrift shop was busy as usual, but Jenny Cairns, the boss, took a few moments for a coffee and a chat. It was nearly twelve when Rob found himself in the city centre. His mobile rang while he was waiting to pay for the new boxes.

"Rob, I'm just running Margaret Spiers across the road to Casualty — young Kim's bashed her head and it looks like it might need stitches. Good job we've got a car each, eh? See you later!"

Rob packed his boxes into the hired car and stood for a moment. There was no need to hurry home; Dad would be a while yet. He would buy some sandwiches and have lunch — and that think he'd been meaning to get round to — in Princes Street Gardens.

It was a mild, sunny day, and Rob wandered along the gardens, soaking up the atmosphere. Tourists and office workers were having lunch, there was the inevitable piper at the gate, the Scott Monument towering above him, and, of course, the castle. Splendid in all weathers and seasons; a piece of history and part of his childhood . . . The lump came back into his throat and he sat down dismally on the nearest bench.

Glasgow was home to his dad, he understood that well now, just as Edinburgh was home to him. Rob became aware that he was upset to be losing his "base" here. He had old school friends he could visit, and the cousins in North Berwick, but it would be just that — a visit. He would never be "coming home" to Edinburgh again.

142

Up The Hill

UP the hill, up the hill!
What shall we find when we reach the top?
A rabbit's round hole, or a wee fairy shop?
A buttercup field, or a thistledown mop?

Behind a tree there might be a bear,
Big, brown and friendly, just waiting there;
We might have a picnic; I'd teach him a game;
And he'd be my best friend once I found out his name.

Up the hill, up the hill!
There's no time to stop for a moment to chat.
I might meet a wizard in his high hat;
Or wave to a witch on her broom with her cat.

I'd look for a dragon and might find one there,
So I'd say, when I'd found him asleep in his lair:
"So sorry to wake you, but since you're awake,
Please do come and join me for tea and a cake!"

Up the hill, up the hill!
There's magic just waiting, I'm willing to bet.
There might be a castle; I can't see it yet,
But I might see it soon, the closer we get.

There might be all sorts of wonderful things:
A bridge to a rainbow; a house that has wings!
We climb and we climb, and it's always a thrill
To be climbing the top of a mountain or hill!

— *Dawn Lawrence.*

143

The one o'clock gun boomed out from the castle, and there were the usual appreciative noises from the tourists in the gardens. Shouts of children's laughter rang out to Rob's left, and he looked round to see two small boys jumping up and down with pleasure, and behind them, Katie, with a pushchair in front of her.

"Come on, you two. The gun made enough noise for now. Let's find a bench and have lunch."

KATIE!" Rob called, suddenly feeling oddly pleased to see her.

She looked round and laughed.

"Great minds think alike," she said, nodding at his packet of sandwiches. "We're just about to picnic, too. Mind if we join you?"

"That'd be great!" Rob said, watching as she produced sandwiches and small cartons of juice for the boys, who sat down on either side of Rob, and a banana for the toddler in the pushchair.

"How's the baby?" Rob asked, remembering the reason for her visit.

"She's much better now, and she's called Amanda, and I'm Danny, and that's Reggie, and that's our sister, Lucy, and my mum and dad are at the hospital, and —"

The older of the boys could hardly get the words out quickly enough. Katie ruffled his hair.

"Whoa, slow down, Dan. Look, here's your grub — tuck in."

Danny giggled and got to work on his chicken sandwich, and Katie grinned at Rob. Her eyes were bright and happy, and there was an air of peace about her that hadn't been there the day before. All was right with her world once more.

Rob swallowed. Katie was special — he suddenly saw that very clearly. She was part of London, but equally at home in Edinburgh — just like him. She was kind, gentle and funny. How could he feel this strongly about someone he'd only just met?

"So it's all OK?" he asked, and she nodded.

"The operation was this morning. Dave said it took all of ten minutes to remove the cyst. Amanda's fine, though she'll have to stay in the hospital for another few days before she's allowed back home."

"I'm glad," Rob said. "You were so worried yesterday."

She looked at him.

"No need to worry now," she said. "But what about you and your dad's removal? You look a bit down."

Rob sighed.

"Dad's happy," he said to Katie. "Looking forward to his new life, and being close to his sister — it's me that's having problems about losing my Edinburgh home.

"Dad grew up in Glasgow, you see, and he's moving back there to a flat

144

close to his sister — just so they can keep an eye on each other."

"But you grew up here," Katie said. "I can understand how you feel. Some places can get right under your skin, can't they?"

Rob nodded. The lump was back in his throat, and he didn't trust himself to speak. Fortunately, the children ensured there was no lull in the conversation.

"Juice!" Lucy yelled, waving her arms in the air.

"Auntie Kate, can we go and chase squirrels afterwards?" Reggie licked his fingers noisily.

"You know Daddy says it's not nice to chase the squirrels," Danny said severely.

"Want a squilley!" Lucy bounced up and down in her chair.

"Careful, Luce," Katie said. "Reggie, we'll go and *count* the squirrels in a minute. How many do you think we'll see?"

"Hundreds!"

THE two little boys immediately jumped up and took their sandwich papers to the bin. Katie grinned at Rob, then put a hand on his arm.

"Hey, are you OK? Edinburgh will still be here any time you want to visit, you know. And your dad sounds like he's happy about the move, and that's the important thing, isn't it?"

Rob nodded. She was right, he knew that. Dad was the most important person in the middle of all this, and he was obviously happy.

Why wouldn't he be, thought Rob — he'll be going home to where he grew up, he'll be living near his sister and making his life easier by down-sizing.

Rob suddenly felt very selfish for giving his dad a hard time about it, and realised that if it was what made his dad happy, then he should be making every effort to be supportive about it.

"Thanks," he said to Katie. "I just got my priorities a bit mixed up. And Glasgow's a great place, too, it's just . . ."

"It isn't Edinburgh!" Katie laughed. "And who said men aren't sentimental!"

Rob patted her hand. He suddenly felt very strongly about Katie, and knew that he had to say something now, before she disappeared out of his life.

"Can I . . . can we maybe . . . would you like to go for a meal some time? Or a coffee, or . . ."

"That would be lovely," Katie said, her eyes shining at him warmly. "Um, I'm here all week, but if you don't have time, then maybe in London . . ."

Rob heaved a sigh of relief. She'd said yes!

He stood up, and grasped the pushchair handle.

"Let's do both," he said, laughing when she nodded, blushing. "Come on, you boys — let's find some squirrels!" ■

ANNIE descended the steps on to the pebbled beach. She had brought the mat and a giant beaker of cappuccino with her, and she was going to relax in the sun for the last part of the afternoon. Later that evening, her two sons and their families would be taking her out for a birthday dinner, and she was looking forward to it.

At the same time, she was finding it unsettling to have notched up yet another year. How is it possible that the years can creep up with such stealth, she wondered. Not so very long ago, she had managed to play down the fact that she'd reached seventy, but now seventy-three had come round she was forced to acknowledge her seventies were well and truly here!

When she was young, she'd not given the process of getting older much thought. She had assumed that by the time you reached the age of seventy you would have gracefully metamorphosed into being an Old Person. But now she understood that was not the way it was at all.

The truth was that when you reached your three-score years and ten, there was no magic transformation in the way you felt about yourself. Your external appearance might have changed, but you were still yourself!

by Judy
Granville.

Ruminating on these thoughts, she picked her way over a beach packed with scores of sun worshippers luxuriating in the glorious Sussex sunshine. Couples on deckchairs, oiled-up bodies prostrate on towels, mothers with tottering toddlers, people relaxing and generally enjoying themselves. Annie had the image of a contented seal colony.

Arriving at her usual spot by the lifeguard's outpost, she unfolded her mat, settled back and took a sip of coffee. This location was a good place from which to observe the lifeguard.

Now there was an indisputably handsome young man, Annie thought. Seated on his elevated chair, surveying his domain — the English Channel and the beaches to the east and to the west — he provided the sunbathing community with a glowing example of masculine youth and vitality.

The lad was not unlike Johnny

Illustration by Martin Baines.

Weissmuller in his heyday. Certainly, he looked the part to rescue a drowning soul with all the glamour of a Hollywood hero. And it was clear he was enjoying his status as guardian of public safety. He obviously loved the attention from the young kids and the pretty teenage girls!

Now that's what I'd like, Annie thought to herself. My own lifesaver to put a splash of colour back into my days!

Annie missed having a man in her life. Her husband, Eric, had died a few years ago. Initially, she'd been bereft, lacking in energy and confidence. But with a little help from her friends and her sons she had survived her loss. Eventually she had grown used to living on her own, and even re-invented her life somewhat.

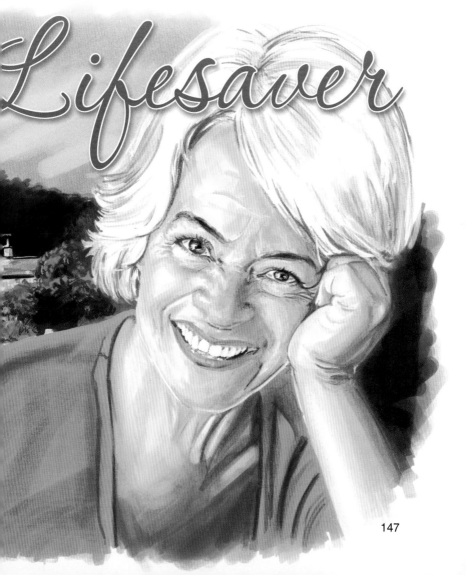

Lifesaver

And she was confident that she was still a contender. Sure, age was taking its toll in some ways: the old joints were a bit stiff in the mornings, for example, and every year there were more lines on her face. But she had kept herself in shape, and — though she said it herself — she looked pretty good! She took pride in the fact that she had only gained a couple of pounds since her twenties. She had resolutely maintained her hair with up-to-date styling, and she always made sure she dressed with flair.

Thankfully there were enough rôle models in the public eye for inspiration: Barbara Windsor, Vanessa Redgrave — even that little old lady, Jane Fonda, was in her seventies now!

ANNIE'S repose in the sunshine did not last long. Her thoughts were interrupted by a bright red Frisbee flying across her line of vision towards the lifeguard. A small boy in blue swimming trunks had playfully lobbed it at his hero to test his reactions.

Unflustered, the invincible lifeguard simply raised a hand to catch it and flipped it back. The boy's face was a picture of delight. He hurled the Frisbee again, and the lifeguard returned it.

Once more the boy threw the Frisbee, and this time it soared high up into the air, wide of the mark. The lifeguard lurched up and over to the side to catch it — but sadly misjudged his balance. Arms flailing, he let out a squawk and toppled over on to the stones. For an undignified moment he sprawled on all fours, groaning.

Annie jumped up and a small crowd instantly gathered around. An elderly man in jogging clothes extended a hand to help the lifeguard up, and Annie gently took hold of his other arm.

As they raised the young man to his feet, it occurred to Annie that there was an irony in the fact that two old folks were rescuing the rescuer! For a brief moment she caught the elderly man's eye. She wondered if the humour had struck him, too, but, politely, neither of them smiled.

"Are you all right?" Annie asked the lifeguard.

He laughed unconvincingly, peering at his forearm.

"Yes, I think so," he said. "But I might have to get this checked out. It could be sprained."

Annie picked up the first-aid box from underneath the lifeguard's chair and offered to make a sling for him. Before long, his arm was bandaged and supported.

"Would you like me to sit here and keep an eye on the beach for the rest of the afternoon?" the man in the jogging suit offered.

"Well, that would be really good," the lifeguard said, as he struggled into his jeans. "If you could. Cheers, mate, thanks. I'll phone my manager and let him know. It's only half an hour till the end of the shift." With that, he hurried off up the beach with the first-aid kit under his good arm.

"That was a neat sling," the distinguished-looking man, now seated in the lifeguard's chair, said.

"Thanks. I did a first-aid course in my voluntary job," Annie replied. She paused to take in this tall, lean man who was regarding her with a cheerful smile. His features seemed familiar to her: short-cropped white hair, calm grey eyes under bushy eyebrows. She thought he was probably in his late sixties.

ARE you a first-aider?" she asked him   .
"Not any more," he said. "I kept up the refresher courses every year, but I let them lapse after I retired in May. Finally, at seventy-three!"

"You're seventy-three?"

"Yes."

"It's my seventy-third birthday today," Annie found herself saying before she had a chance to think about it.

"Really! Nineteen thirty-seven was a vintage year!" he said.

There was something about him she recognised.

"Have I met you somewhere before?" she asked.

"No, but I come here for a dip almost every day, so you might have seen me around," he said. "I've often seen you on this beach. You come here in the afternoons, don't you?"

"That's right."

He reached down, holding out his hand.

"Sydney," he said.

"Annie." She shook it.

He reached into a pocket for his wallet, took out a business card, and quaintly handed it to her. It read, *SYDNEY STRUTT — Sailing Solutions*, followed by a mobile number.

"I owe that lifeguard a favour," he said with a grin. "Giving me the opportunity to introduce myself to you."

"Well, I expect he'd rather have done without the accident!" Annie said. "So how's it feel, up there in the hot seat?"

Sydney took a look out to sea and across the beach.

"The sea's calm, so with luck no-one's going to get into trouble out there this afternoon. The main danger in these parts is the flying Frisbees!"

Annie giggled.

"No sign of the boy who threw it!" she said. "I think he scarpered, quick!"

"Yes, he left his Frisbee behind, look!" There it was, by the lifeguard's chair.

Annie was finding it easy to engage in conversation with Sydney, and she stood by the chair chatting with him for a while. Gradually, he told her a little about his background. He had lived all his life in Yorkshire, but when his wife had died three years before, his son, Mark, had suggested he move to

Shoreham to be near him and the family.

"At first I declined," he told Annie. "But after a while it occurred to me that I might enjoy the challenge of a fresh start, so in the end I took the plunge. It's turned out to be a new lease of life down here. And one bonus is that being a few degrees further south makes a difference when you're in the sea. You do notice that it's slightly warmer."

Annie responded with a few details of her own life story, which Sydney took in with respectful interest. An hour slipped by, and they continued to talk.

When she finally looked around, the sun was almost touching the sea and the sky was glowing coral and pink. She looked at her watch.

"Well, I must go," she said, folding up her mat.

"Let me ask you something, Annie," Sydney began. "Do you like dancing? I've recently discovered that the Grand Hotel does a high tea with dancing and champagne once a month."

"Well . . ."

"I imagine you're a natural on the dance floor!"

She gave him a sidelong glance.

"Would that be flattery, at all?"

He laughed.

"It would, but I'm right, aren't I? I'd be a fool not to ask you. Don't say anything now, just give it some thought, will you? You have my phone number."

"OK, I'll give it some thought. But I'm a bit rusty . . ." She realised she had already mentally accepted the invitation. She looked at his card. "By the way, what are 'Sailing Solutions' exactly?"

"It's the name of my sailing consultancy. I was running courses till I moved down here."

"It seems you've had a good friendship with the sea all your life," Annie said.

"That's true," Sydney replied, his eyes twinkling. "I've even done some voluntary work as a lifeguard in my spare time."

✳   ✳   ✳   ✳

Annie strolled along the sea front, and turned to look back across the beach towards the lifeguard's station. She focused on the figure in the chair in the distance.

The sun was now below the horizon, and the crowds were beginning to pack up and drift off.

As she stood leaning against the promenade rail, she had a sense of something having shifted in her destiny. Perhaps coming to the beach today had been fate. She was supposed to meet Sydney and that poor lifeguard was supposed to fall off his chair! Sometimes, she smiled to herself, fate could be both kind and cruel! ■

Winkle Street, Calbourne, Isle of Wight

*T*HE *first time I came across*
*Winkle Street in Calbourne, I wondered whether or not it might
just be the prettiest street in Britain! What a charming place, and your
artist managed to capture it on just the sort of glorious May day that
my wife and I had when we were there.*

*I was won over to the area completely when we visited Upper
Calbourne Mill. It was lovely to see the six-metre-high water wheel still
in action, and we had a delightful afternoon wandering around the
garden, having a cup of tea and then just ambling leisurely through the
village.*

An unforgettable day in an unforgettable location.

— Mr M.P., Southampton.

J. CAMPBELL KERR.

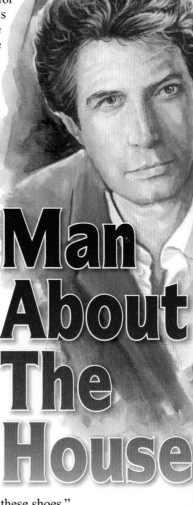

IT was my sister's wedding day. My daughter was being a bridesmaid for the first time, my husband was standing around looking like "Man at C&A", and my two sons were driving me up the wall.

Now, weddings are a girlie thing, for girls of all ages. So, as expected, four-year-old Molly had been in a state of excitement these past few weeks, in the build-up to Auntie Sara's wedding.

But now, on the big day, there she was, as good as gold, watching TV, sitting very still in case she disturbed the ringlets in her long, flaxen hair.

No, it was the boys who were giving me problems — all three of them. Standing in the kitchen doorway, six-year-old Julian was blocking my way into the hall. Hands dug deep inside his dressing-gown pockets, he looked the picture of misery.

"Julian," I said, squeezing past him. "You're not walking into church with a football under your arm, and that's final."

Julian's chin nearly hit the floor.

"Oh, Muuum . . ."

"Mum," ten-year-old Chris echoed, emerging from the living-room with a school shoe in each hand. "Can't I wear my trainers? I hate these shoes."

"Chris, for the last time, you're not going to a wedding in your trainers."

"We could leave them in the car, Steph," Paul, my husband, said, ambling down the stairs. "He could always put them on later."

"Can I leave my football in the car, then?" Julian asked, not missing a trick.

"You tell them, Paul," I said, heading up the stairs, fuming at the unfairness of it all. There he was, looking very handsome in his wedding outfit — slate-grey suit and pink shirt to show off his blue eyes — and he wasn't going anywhere for another two hours.

152

Man About The House

And here I was, due out in less than an hour, still in my dressing-gown. Thank goodness my sister didn't want page-boys . . .

YOU look nice," the dutiful husband said, when I walked into the living-room forty-five minutes later to find everyone sitting around watching TV with Molly. What was going on here? Was I the only one going to a wedding today?

As for my outfit, yes, I was really pleased with it — a coral and buttercup-coloured dress with a cropped matching jacket.

Being dark-haired, like the boys, I could always get away with bold colours.

On my way out with Molly, I turned to look at my three men, who had followed me into the hallway. Julian, still in his dressing-gown, was looking up at me pitifully.

Illustration by Mark Viney.

by Brenda Joy.

"It'll be fine, Julian," I said, bending to kiss his cheek. "Daddy will sort you out. I've got to get Molly to Gran's. Auntie Sara will be waiting for her."

"It's down to you now, Paul," I said as I opened the front door. "Just remember the magic word — anticipation."

I was just getting into the taxi when the final question was shot down the path after me.

"Steph . . . where are Julian's clothes?"

"He'll show you," I called back, feeling quite guilty, as though I was abandoning my sons into the care of an incompetent.

How will they cope without me, I wondered as the taxi pulled away. How will the boys look when they turn up at the church? Will they be on

153

time? Even worse — will they even get there?

And just think, I'll be going through this all over again in a couple of months' time when my friend Myra gets married. OK, so Molly won't be a bridesmaid then, but everything else will be the same . . .

The problem is, like a lot of women, I do too much for my family and then, of course, they come to expect it and take me for granted.

All they have to do is turn up. And I don't just mean at the wedding, I mean on a daily basis. None of them would ever be on time anywhere if I wasn't behind them.

And the questions! I still couldn't believe what Julian said when I first told him he couldn't take his football into the church.

"Do we have to go to the church?" he asked. "Can't we just go straight to the party?"

I sat the two boys down then, and explained to them about Auntie Sara's wedding ceremony being an important family occasion, and that today we would be making memories we would keep for the rest of our lives. I was speaking from experience. I'd never forgotten the family weddings I'd been to over the years . . .

And what did the helpful husband do while all this was going on? He laughed. It was the "missing out the church" bit that did it.

As the taxi sped towards my mother's house, I permitted myself a little smile. Well, my charming, handsome, unbelievably laid-back husband would be laughing on the other side of his face . . . round about now . . .

*　　*　　*　　*

So, there I was, a couple of hours later, sitting in the church with all the other guests, awaiting the arrival of the bridal party. Of course, I was also waiting for my three men, who finally made it, just minutes before the bride.

"Couldn't find anywhere to park," Paul hissed, as he slid into the pew beside me, followed by the boys, whose expressions were somewhere between bewilderment and relief.

They both looked very smart in their new outfits — jazzy waistcoats, dark trousers and long-sleeved shirts in pale gold, though I did notice a dubious-looking stain on one of Julian's sleeves. I was just about to make enquiries, when the organist signalled the arrival of the bride.

"Just in time," I said pleasantly. "Another few minutes and you would have been pageboys."

"You don't know the half of it," Paul muttered. "You wouldn't believe the job I've had getting Julian ready."

Wouldn't I?

After the ceremony, as everyone posed for a group photograph in the church garden, I was just about to ask about Julian's shirt, when Chris piped up.

154

"Julian spilled orange juice on his shirt. You should have seen it, Mum. It was soaking wet."

"Could've been worse," Mr Confident said, running his fingers through his hair. "Could've been blackcurrant juice or cola."

"Dad dried it with your hairdryer," Chris continued. "And we looked everywhere for the new ties . . . they'd fallen down the back of the settee . . ."

"Yes, thank you, Chris," the head of the family said in a voice so petulant, it could have almost been Julian's.

For a few seconds there, my easy-going husband had a look in his eyes I hadn't seen before . . . on him at least. I'd seen it often enough in the mirror myself. It's called stress.

My initial response was to gloat. He'd just had a taste of what my life was like on a daily basis. But, funnily enough, now that I'd proved my point, I felt sorry for him.

AS we posed for a photograph of the bride's family, a little hand slid into mine.

"We missed you, Mum," Julian said. "Dad's all right and everything, but it's not the same without you."

Just as I was giving Julian a hug, Chris leaned in from the other side.

"Sorry about the trainers, Mum. These shoes are OK."

As we stood there — me, my three men and my little girl — I hoped that in the future, whenever I looked at this photograph, I would remember how I was feeling right now . . . how my heart was so full of love . . .

"Come on now, smile," I said, looking straight ahead. "This is one for the family album."

The next photograph was of the bride and bridesmaids. The threatening tears finally brimmed over as I watched Molly take her place in front of my sister, looking like a little wood nymph in her pale green dress and floral crown.

Another lovely photo, I thought, dabbing my eyes. Another lovely memory to look back on when Molly's older . . . when we're all older . . .

I've never forgotten the first time I was a bridesmaid at my auntie's wedding. I felt so special, so pretty . . . like a six-year-old fairy princess.

Sometimes, when I look at that photograph, I can hardly believe it's me. And I wonder, what was she thinking about then, that little girl . . .

Photographs. They're a sort of back-up for the memory — holidays, Christmas, weddings — all going back over the years . . .

We're all younger and full of hope, not knowing what life has in store for us. Yet there we are, all together, as we were back then, in the photographs, and in my memories.

"We're going to start helping you more, aren't we, boys?" Mr Supportive said, as Chris and Julian nodded in agreement — obviously the result of a good talking to. "And I see what you mean about anticipation. When Julian asked for a drink of cola this morning, I gave him orange juice instead, and saved the day . . ."

So he did listen — sometimes! It just got better and better. And the bottom line was they did appreciate me, even if it had taken a stressful morning to make them realise it.

WHEN the photographs were finished, we all made our way back to the cars. But as the glowing bride and her new husband walked towards their car, I caught sight of something on the pavement, a few yards ahead of them, and suddenly everything seemed to go into slow motion . . .

Quick, somebody do something, I felt like shouting. Was I the only one who could see it? The can of cola — upturned and spewing out a torrent of dark, fizzy liquid.

Apparently not, because suddenly my husband — the new man — shot out in front of the bride and kicked the offending can to one side. Then, calm as you like, he directed his sister-in-law and her flowing white dress away from the sticky puddle and towards her waiting carriage.

There were a few cheers for this show of gallantry — somewhere between Sir Walter Raleigh and David Beckham — by the father-of-three who had so obviously missed his vocation.

"Well, how was that for anticipation?" Sir Walter Beckham said as we got into the car.

"Not bad," I replied, trying not to laugh. "You're getting there." In fact, you've been quite impressive, I thought, as the seeds of a plan began to form in my mind . . .

As we drove along, Molly, who'd decided to travel to the reception with us, gave us a big sigh. Then, as old as the hills, she made a declaration.

"I think I'll remember today for ever. Will you remember today for ever, Mummy?"

We'd stopped at the traffic lights and I could feel Paul's eyes on me, waiting for my reply. Smiling, I turned to face him before I did.

"Yes, darling, I certainly will."

Oh, well, I thought. He's really tried today. And if he keeps this up he could soon be ready for the next stage in childcare — a twenty-four-hour tour of duty, tending to the needs of two budding football stars and a four-year-old wood nymph.

And that would mean I could actually consider going to Myra's hen party next month — an overnight trip to Blackpool. Of course, this would be followed a few weeks later by her wedding — another family occasion, another set of photographs, and even more memories to be made . . . ■

Batteries

I'VE been recharging batteries,
Replacing others, too,
Technology is wonderful —
So much that we can do.
But here's another good idea,
I'm sure you will agree,
An energising battery
Designed for you and me.

Then we could use it when we're low,
Or when we're feeling down,
And maybe buy another one
When we go into town.
I hope some bright-eyed scientist
Will one day see the light,
And make us all a battery
For charging through the night.

— *Iris Hesselden.*

Willie Shand.

157

We'll Meet Again

IT was cold that afternoon. It looked as though someone had hauled a great slab over our grimy little town, and the odd tiny snowflake spiralled down in the frozen stillness. It was like the whole world was holding its breath, waiting for someone.

I took a last look at my baby brother, Terry, in his cot and gave my mum a hug as she stood with her arms in a bowl of washing-up water, pausing from soaping the dinner plates. She bent down and kissed my forehead.

"Hurry up, love," she said. "You'll be late."

"Be good," she added, as I was pulling the front door shut. "Grandad might have a surprise for you on Saturday." My grandad lived with my auntie Emily at the top of Tower Street, by the allotments.

I was six, maybe seven (Terry was born when I was six), and I was allowed to walk the short way, morning and afternoon, to and from the little redbrick school on the hill; nobody thought anything about it in those days, the late Fifties.

A three-leg zig-zag took me down to the end of Inkerman Terrace where we lived, along Alma Street and Balaclava Street, and up the steep cinder track that led to the school.

Late or not, there would be things to see on the way, and I paid a childish homage to each one every school day. There was the great humming cotton-mill on Balaclava Street, where my dad worked, built of the same shiny red bricks as the school, but more smoke-blackened; it seemed to throb and sigh, and the smell of hot machinery wafted from fluff-choked circular fans set in the windows.

Farther along Balaclava Street I would stretch up on tiptoe to look down into a shiny Austin car that was usually parked outside the mill's wages office, thrilled by the leather seats and the polished wooden dashboard with its clocks and dials.

My next stop would be the contract laundry where a dirty-faced, bad-tempered man in a filthy boiler suit and an old Army beret shovelled boiler-coke around the yard. You could also glimpse rosy-cheeked women and girls wrestling with steaming snakes of white linen through the little side-door, which was always open for their comfort.

The cinder track up to the school was a wonderland in spring; its black surface was scarred by canyons down which rainwater would rush and gurgle in torrents — rivers which you could dam with your wellies until the water slopped over their tops.

158

I was late. There were no other children in sight, and I felt a little thrill of anxiety. I stepped up my pace a bit, feeling the tops of my wellingtons chafing against bare legs, and I scratched my chin through the wool of my balaclava, which always tormented it.

I'D just turned into the appropriately named Balaclava Street and gone a few feet when something in the doorway of a back yard caught my eye. Down in the corner, barely outlined against the dirty, peeling green paintwork of the door, was a tiny, grubby-looking bird, huddled against the cold with his feathers all fluffed up and his eyes closed.

I gave a little gasp. I bent down to look more closely and then took him carefully in my gloved hands. He opened his eyes for a second and a flake of snow landed right on his little domed head. He didn't seem like a sparrow or a wild bird . . .

I'm a ditherer, always have been, and I dithered then. I can see myself, all

by Laura Weekes.

Illustration by
David McAllister.

those years ago, hopping from one foot to the other, not sure what to do to help the little creature.

I looked up and down the street, which was empty of people, and could see that the snowflakes were multiplying and moving around on a breeze that had sprung up; the sky was now black. Behind me, the factory moaned ominously.

I put the little bird back in position in the scant shelter of the doorway. What were my options? Run home with him? Take him to school?

I did neither.

"Wait there, I'll be back soon," I said and sprinted along the street towards the school.

I trotted past the shiny car without glancing at it. The boilerman in the coke yard leant on his shovel and spat, eyeing me without interest as I flashed by, and I noticed that the laundry door was shut; that's how cold it was.

As I turned the corner, by the rusty chain-link fence, and was about to start up the track, I looked back, still in an agony of indecision.

I could see two figures in the distance, making their way down Tower Street. One of them was Grandad. Should I run back and tell him about the little bird?

I couldn't make out who the other man was, for the snow was thicker now, and starting to dance and swirl in the air. Fear of being late made me run on, up the cinder track and across the tarmac playground into school.

I suffered a thoroughly miserable afternoon, with the guilt of my foolishness and indecision making me ache all over. If the little bird could just hang on I'd pick him up on the way back and run home to my mum with him.

Would he still be there? The street had been empty, there'd been no-one about to harm him. He'd sit and wait patiently for me. Wouldn't he?

I LOVED my teacher, Miss Barnes. She was young and pretty, and kind. She'd give you a hug if you did something well, or needed encouragement, or were upset. Teachers could do that then. I wanted to tell her about the little bird, organise a rescue mission, but I didn't.

I was on the verge of tears all afternoon, and very quiet. I could feel a sob rising in my throat every now and again, and fought to control it. I thought of nothing else but the pathetic little creature shivering in the doorway, and prayed that he would hold on.

I was so distracted that I sat through the Brer Rabbit story at the end of the afternoon and didn't hear a single word. I was in a brightly lit classroom which smelled of books and Plasticine and poster paint, with my favourite teacher, and the little bird was out there where daylight had now gone, and snowflakes were whispering against the window-glass and falling away without melting.

160

I loved the Brer Rabbit stories and I loved Miss Barnes, in a childish, misty way, and if she'd showed me some special kindness that afternoon I would have dissolved in tears and confessed. But I covered my tracks well, fought back the urge to cry, and managed to get through what seemed like an eternity.

As soon as school finished I was halfway down the cinder track before the bell had stopped ringing. There was a cluster of parents standing by the gate, waiting for the tiniest pupils, but I flew past them and down the hill, feet crunching on the frozen cinders, and was soon turning on to Balaclava Street by the chain-link fence and the steaming laundry.

I ran like I'd never run before, past the gleaming blue car, now no colour at all under a street light, past the coke yard and the ring and scrape of the grumpy man's shovel.

Ahead, on the right, lay the doorway, partly illuminated by the light from the factory windows opposite. The air was filled with whirling flakes and the smell of hot oil. It was getting colder.

I approached it with a knocking heart, ready to do my good deed. I would run home with the little bird to my mum.

I could see it clearly — me eating my tea, Dad smoking a cigarette and reading his newspaper, and the bird in a cardboard box by the fire, snuggled down into a nest of torn newspapers, perhaps with a saucer of water and some seed.

I stood in front of the doorway. It was bare. I looked, and looked again, not believing my eyes. I widened my search, along the bottom of the wall in either direction, up a side entry on the right, among the tall, dead weeds, in this doorway and that, frantically.

BY now other children were hurrying along Balaclava Street, some with parents in tow, bathed in the lights from the factory, heads down in the cold wind and anxious to get home to tea.

As I was coming out of the side entry for another look along the street, Mrs Bright, with her son, Mike, was crossing to my side. She stopped, and looked suspiciously at me.

"Haven't you got a home to go to, David?" she asked.

I nodded without saying anything, now on the verge of losing my battle with the tears that were again welling up inside me. I turned in the direction of Alma Street and home.

"Run along," Mrs Bright shouted after me. "There's a good boy!"

That evening was torment. After tea, the scene in our poky kitchen-cum-living-room was as usual — my mum washing the crockery, Terry gurgling in his pram, my dad staring into the fire with a Woodbine on the go, the blue smoke drifting up to mingle with the clean washing which was airing on a rack suspended from the ceiling.

Later on we watched "Take Your Pick", a popular quiz show. The only thing missing was the box by the fire, with its precious inhabitant. I was very quiet, but no-one seemed to notice, and at the appointed time I went up to bed with the theme music from the TV Western "Gunsmoke" following me up the stairs.

I nearly told my mum when she came up to tuck me in, but didn't, and I lay awake for a long time, watching the strip of light on my bedroom wall which came from a street-light outside.

Perhaps the little bird could survive the night and I'd find him in the morning. I'd look carefully on my way to school. I comforted myself with that thought and then fell asleep, exhausted.

The next day my hopes were dashed. The light which came through the gap in my curtains was bright, strange and other-worldly. A layer of snow covered everything outside, and it had frozen in the night.

What would normally have brought joy just deepened my misery. Our dustbin, with a six-inch layer on its lid, looked like an iced bun, and icicles hung from the gutters outside my window.

I gobbled my breakfast and hurried to Balaclava Street, ignoring my schoolbound friends, who were dawdling and mucking around in the snow. But there was no sign of the little bird.

There were some tracks in the snow around the doorway, but they were too big, and whatever bird had made them was healthy and strong, not weak and poorly. There were also shoe-prints; perhaps someone else had found him.

As the rest of the week passed I began to feel a bit better, although I didn't forget about the little bird. But Miss Barnes and Brer Rabbit stories at school distracted me, and I looked forward to seeing Grandad at the weekend, partly because Mum had said that he had a surprise for me, so the pain was eased a bit.

ON Saturday afternoon Grandad came to collect me and Terry, and we walked round to my auntie Emily's in Tower Street; he pushed Terry in the pram, and I held on to the handle. The hard snow squeaked under our wellingtons in the bright sunshine, and the factory lay silent on our left.

Grandad struggled with the pram through the rutted snow, and had to stop to get his breath once or twice. He'd once worked in the mill, but the cotton had got into his chest and now he coughed and wheezed. But he never complained.

At Auntie Emily's, the pram was manhandled into the narrow hall, and then Grandad, who didn't seem to be able to wait, grabbed my hand and led me through to the tiny living-room at the back.

"Come and look at this!" he said.

The back room was a bit gloomy after the snow and the sunshine outside, but what stood out was a gleaming chrome birdcage with one of those clear, plastic birdbaths clamped to it. The cage had pride of place on the dining table.

I couldn't make out what was inside the bath, but I could hear an enthusiastic chirping and a lot of splashing.

I peered through the cage and gave a cry of astonishment. It was the grubby little bird, now a lot cleaner. He was standing in an inch of tepid water and doing a little jig in front of a tiny mirror, chirping fit to burst.

ALL the tension and unhappiness of the week seemed to rise up inside me again, and with tears running down my cheeks and a shuddering sob I turned and hugged the nearest adult, which happened to be my mum, who'd followed us up the road and had come in without me noticing.

"Hey, hey," she said, pulling me tightly against her. "What's the matter, love? Ooh, you are a funny little thing!"

"What's the matter, lad, don't you like him?" Grandad said. "He's a budgie."

I pulled away from Mum and nodded vigorously, wiping my wet cheeks at the same time.

"I do like him," I said, between sobs, when I could speak, and then started crying again.

"He's a lucky little perisher," Grandad said. "He got out when your auntie was paying the coalman. Me and your uncle Bill spent all Tuesday afternoon looking for him. A cat could've had him.

"It was nearly dark when we found him in a back alley by the mill. He were that mucky he looked like he'd been up somebody's chimney."

My sobs had subsided a bit now, and I peered into the cage again. The little bird, whose name was Billy, it turned out, hopped out of the bath and did a little waddling hornpipe walk along his perch towards me.

Looking me straight in the eye, or so it seemed, he bobbed up and down in great excitement, and a burbling, warbling series of chirps came from his beak. He seemed, in his own way, to be saying something very important.

"Hey, he's really taken to you, David," my mum said, plucking gently at the top of my balaclava.

I was absolutely convinced that the little green bird recognised me. I still am to this day, fifty years later. And although not fluent in budgie, I was sure that he was forgiving me.

And, you know, that made me feel a whole lot better. ∎

How Does Your Garden Grow?

JAKE HAZELDEW trudged along the pebbled path to the glasshouses, his breath clouding in the frosty dawn air. As an apprentice gardener on the estate, it fell to Jake to keep the stoke-house fire stoked up and make sure the temperature was right in the buildings. It was a mucky task and not Jake's favourite, but there was respite afterwards in entering the fragrant warmth of the glasshouses and spending a short time out of the wintry cold.

It was very still in the garden. Even the birds were quiet; the robin that usually followed Jake on his rounds was not yet up and about.

As he reached the end of the path, a quiver of movement in the viburnum bushes that flanked the high boundary wall pulled him up short. Even as he watched, a hand appeared and plucked off some of the creamy-white blooms.

"Hey!" Jake shouted, springing forward. "Who's there? What are you up to?"

There was a stifled yelp of surprise, a panicked rustle of branches, and from behind the bushes, a girl emerged, looking a little shamefaced.

She was small and trim and wore a thick woollen shawl over her gown of dark-blue homespun. Seeing her rosy face and bright brown eyes, Jake was immediately put in mind of his friend, the robin.

"I . . . I wasn't doing any harm," she stammered. "I only wanted a few blossoms for a pot-pourri I'm making."

Jake saw that she was clutching a wicker trug which contained an assortment of tiny larch cones, beech nuts and other woodland pickings.

"This is private land," he said. "You're not supposed to be here. How did you get in, anyway?"

"Through the side gate . . ." The girl hesitated, looking nervous. "When the maids go out on a Saturday night, they get one of the footmen to leave the gate unlocked. Then they can get the last train back and come home . . . a bit later."

A smile curved Jake's lips. Slipping in after hours was common practice amongst the apprentices, too.

"Promise you won't say anything?" the girl pleaded. "The pot-pourri is for my mistress, for Christmas. There aren't many flowers to be had

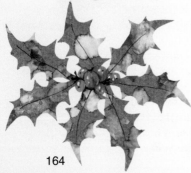

164

Illustration by
Patricia Ludlow.

by Pamela
Kavanagh.

at this time of year and these looked so tempting from the road."

Jake's heart softened. She was such a pretty thing and he could understand the temptation.

"They make a Christmas pot-pourri up at the manor," he said, in a more friendly tone. "It gets put in little dishes to scent the air in the rooms. We grow roses for it."

"Roses make you think of summer," the girl said, nodding.

"We have them in the winter as well here, in the rose house," Jake told her. "And if I don't make tracks and stoke up the boiler it'll be out, and then I'll have the gaffer to answer to! Come on, miss, I'll see you to the gate."

They set off, Jake pulling his jacket closer about him against the cold. It was missing a few buttons, and this morning he was regretting it.

"You'll catch your death going around like that," the girl said, noticing. "What happened to the buttons?"

"They came off a while back — and I'm not much good with a needle and thread. Mam'll sew them back on when it's my day off."

"I'll do it for you, if you like," she offered shyly. "As a thank-you — you know, for being so understanding about the snowberry flowers."

"Viburnum," Jake said. "That's its proper name."

"Really?" She looked impressed. "We call it snowberry where I come from, 'cos it blooms with the snow. Will I do your coat for you? You'll be a lot warmer."

"That's true," Jake said. "That would be really kind of you . . ."

They had reached the narrow wrought-iron gate in the wall.

"You haven't told me your name."

"It's Holly Willis. I'm from the house by the bridge. And you're Jake, aren't you? I've heard them shouting for you when I've been walking past."

"Aye, well, that's what it's like to be an apprentice — you're always at someone's beck and call."

"Do you mind that, Jake? Don't you wish you were free to please yourself?"

"I shall be one day," Jake replied. "Once I've served my apprenticeship I'll be a journeyman. Then I shall apply for whatever job takes my fancy."

Promising to come back the following day to deal with his coat, she slipped out through the gateway and vanished in a flurry of blue skirts into the frosted woodland beyond.

*   *   *   *

Next day, Holly sped along the woodland path, the sewing items safely in the deep pocket of her dress.

She was later than she'd intended. Tabitha the cat had not turned up for her breakfast and, since the mistress doted on her pet, Holly had spent a good fifteen minutes searching for her.

At last she had come across the miscreant in the hayloft above the stable — with four mewling, newborn kittens. What a time of year to be born!

Pink-cheeked and breathless, Holly hurried out of the wood to see Jake's tall, spare figure by the gate.

"Thank goodness," she gasped. "I was afraid you may have gone. Have you brought the buttons with you?"

Jake produced them, and blowing on her hands to warm them, Holly proceeded to sew them back on to the coat. As she wielded the needle and thread she explained her reason for being late, telling him about the new arrivals and how she knew her mistress would go to great lengths to find good homes for them all in due course.

"I'm very fond of my mistress. She's quite young and not a bit stuffy —

we're more like friends, really," she confided happily.

"Times have changed since the old Queen went," Jake commented. "With the coming of the railways, the world seems a smaller place. Rules have relaxed a lot, too."

"That's what my mistress says. She values her independence greatly — taking herself off and renting a house for a taste of country living, as she has, would never have been accepted at one time."

The shawl had slipped from her bent head and the scent of her hair drifted on the air. It was fresh, like springtime.

Jake swallowed hard.

"Thought you weren't from hereabouts," he remarked. "Have you come from far away?"

"From Winchester. We brought a small household with us. Just Cook and Jenkins, the groom . . . and there's myself, of course. A girl comes up from the village to do the cleaning and that's it." Holly smiled.

"My lady loves it here. I expect we shall remain for quite some time."

"Do you like being a lady's maid?"

"Why, yes. I'm very fortunate in my mistress. What about you? Is your boss good to work for?"

"Not bad. He knows horticulture and that's the main thing. My bugbear's the dratted stove!"

Jake pulled a comical face and made her laugh.

"Poor Jake! I don't much like doing the fires, either. I'd sooner make pot-pourri any day. It's fun adding all the bits and bobs. I hope mine will be ready in time."

"You've still got three weeks till Christmas," Jake said encouragingly. "You might add some orange and lemon peel for a festive mix — that's what they do up at the house."

"What a good idea," Holly said, snapping off the thread with small white teeth. "There were are — all done."

HE slipped the coat back on and Holly buttoned it up for him with nimble fingers and smiled up at him.

Jake felt his heart quicken.

"Thanks," he said gruffly, and, delving into his pocket, he brought out a slim package.

"Thought this might come in handy. It's out of my own bit of garden. We all get a patch of ground to grow stuff, see."

Holly peeped inside.

"Oh . . . Jake . . ." It contained sprigs of scented herbs and the pink petals of hellebore. "Thank you. It's exactly what I need."

"Don't forget the peel. Oh, and add a stick of cinnamon. Can you come by them?"

"I'm not sure about the cinnamon."

"Leave it with me. I'll see what I can do," Jake said. "I'll have to go now. Thank you, Holly."

Holly listened to his footsteps crunching away over the pebbled path. There was something stoical and enduring about Jake.

He was like one of the trees in the grounds of the manor; tall, bending with the wind but strong enough to survive its battering.

Holly sang happily to herself as she tripped homeward through the little wood, the unexpected gift stowed carefully away in her pocket.

✳   ✳   ✳   ✳

Jake slammed the door of the stoke-house stove and stood still for a moment, thinking.

Something magical had happened when Holly had smiled at him. The world had suddenly seemed a brighter place, as if the sun had come out and dusted the white-frosted garden with gold.

Garden Glories!

NEWCOMERS to the gardening world, these compact Hydrangeas Tivoli produce an abundance of showy bi-coloured flowers between June and September.

Whether you want to plant them in pots or at the centre of a border, you couldn't ask for more from these reliable hydrangeas that will flower year after year in ever-increasing numbers.

With extravagant giant mop-heads of up to 20cm (8") in diameter, you're going to love showing off these white-edged, lilac beauties — and telling your friends and family exactly what they are!

"Day-dreaming, Jake?"

Jake looked up to see his boss standing in the doorway. The head gardener, known to the apprentices as the gaffer, had a weathered face and shrewd blue eyes that did not miss much.

"Just thinking," Jake said.

"Oh, aye — thinking, is it?" The gaffer quirked a knowing brow. "I've seen that look before. It generally leads to wedding bells and a cottage on the estate."

"Not this time," Jake said firmly, pulling himself together with an effort. "Not till I've made my way as a journeyman."

"Your apprenticeship comes to an end next Easter, doesn't it?" The gaffer paused, then came in and pulled the door shut. "Wanted a word about that, lad. You wouldn't consider stopping on here? There'll be a position as under-gardener going next year. I thought to recommend you. That's if you're interested."

Jake stared at his boss, his mind spinning. He was honoured to be offered the post, but had set his heart on seeing what lay beyond the place where he had been born and raised.

"Want to think about it?" his boss suggested. "Leave it till after Christmas,

then let me know what you've decided."

"I'll do that," Jake agreed. "My thanks, sir."

"Right, then. You'd best get on and check those glasshouses. There was a hard frost last night."

As he made the rounds of the benches, Jake marvelled that the pipes running underneath could keep the frost at bay so efficiently. He only wished there was a better way of maintaining it! Stoking up was one task he would not regret handing over when his term of apprenticeship was over.

When the job was done, he headed off for the kitchens and the breakfast that awaited. While he was there, he remembered the cinnamon, and cajoled Cook into giving him a couple of sticks.

"What d'you want this for?" she enquired, mystified.

Cook was fond of Jake — they all were, below stairs — and his affinity with plants was legendary.

Jake gave her a wink.

"Secret," he said and, tucking the item into his top pocket, he went out into the cold again.

L ATER, in the garden room, making up garlands of evergreen for the house, he noticed some bundles of small summer flowers which had been hung to dry on the rafters above.

"Mind if I take some of those?" Jake asked his boss.

"What, the helichrysum?" The gaffer looked in doubt at the froth of pretty, papery blue and pink blooms. "You're never putting them in the decoration?"

"No," Jake replied, but he didn't elaborate.

"Help yourself," the gaffer said with another of those looks that made Jake feel a tad disconcerted. All at once, life wasn't clear cut any more and he was at a loss to know why.

When he was sure there was no-one else about, Jake put the flowers and the cinnamon in an old cloth cap that had seen better days and placed it by a holly bush just outside the gate, where Holly would be sure to find them.

Next morning, the items had gone and in their place was a slab of home-made treacle toffee. Smiling, Jake popped a piece into his mouth and

169

chewed as he went to tackle the stove. It was his favourite, as it happened, and it tasted very good indeed.

It continued from there. Every couple of days, he'd leave some small offering in the cap and receive another in return. He thought he might run out of ideas, but it never seemed to happen. Flower heads or berries for the pot-pourri, a twist of spice for added fragrance, a pretty ribbon . . . there was always an item he thought she might like.

Holly's gifts were equally thoughtful. A slice of gingerbread, sticky and sweet, a russet apple, a few nuts . . . always something to cheer him up and take the chore out of that first early morning task.

"You sound in high spirits, Jake," one of the other apprentices remarked.

They were building a cold frame and Jake was whistling as he worked.

Jake grinned but made no reply. It seemed he was always in good spirits these days.

Ever since Holly had come into his world, things had subtly changed. Up until then, the garden had been his sole vision, but now there was Holly.

He had begun lingering by the gate in the hope of catching her, but he never did.

No doubt there was some whispering going on behind his back; little went unobserved in a big house. But Jake didn't care. Let them whisper!

ONE evening, when Jake and the other apprentices were sitting round the bothy fire drinking a cup of bedtime cocoa, the subject of the Yuletide Supper cropped up. The feast for the below stairs and outdoor staff was held by tradition on Christmas Eve. There would be dancing and entertainment. Every boy would take his girl.

"Will you be bringing anyone, Jake?" one of the crowd asked.

"That'd be telling," Jake said.

He felt his cheekbones grow warm. He had assumed this to be his last Yuletide Supper at the house, but now he wasn't so sure. He still had not said anything to the gaffer about his offer.

Jake found himself in a dilemma. For all he knew, Holly was like her mistress, one of the new independent spirits that were cropping up everywhere — she might not want to be seen with a garden boy with grandiose ideas of becoming a journeyman.

After a lot of thought, he decided to write her a note, asking her to meet him, and take it from there.

The following morning, however, when Jake went to put his carefully penned message in the old cloth cap, he found his previous day's gift still there. It was a fragrant twist of sandalwood raspings which he'd gone to some lengths to obtain from the still-room maid.

Fighting back a wave of disappointment, Jake told himself that Holly must have been busy — likely she would turn up later, he thought, and went on his way.

But disappointment faced him each time he returned to the spot throughout the day.

When at length dusk crept across the garden and still there was no sign of Holly, Jake gave up. Clearly she wasn't coming. She must have grown tired of playing games, and who could blame her? A perky girl like that must surely have better things to do.

∗　　∗　　∗　　∗

Holly gave the earthenware crock a vigorous shake, pulled off the stopper and inhaled deeply.

Mmm . . . the pot-pourri smelled of December woodland and festive delights. Wistfully, she tipped a small amount of the pot-pourri into a muslin bag, tying it with the red ribbon from Jake. If only his eyes had lit up the same way for her as they did when he spoke of his beloved garden.

If only.

What a babe he must have thought her, with her offerings of gingerbread and toffee. Whatever had possessed her?

Fortunately, she had come to her senses before she had made herself look too foolish and decided that she wouldn't be leaving any more gifts for the young man, however nice his eyes were.

Wondering what to do with the rest of the scented petals, for she had made far too much, she put the stopper back on the crock.

At that moment, the clatter and rattle of the pony and trap heralded the return of her mistress from taking afternoon tea at the manor.

Putting the crock aside, Holly hastened down the stairs.

"Hey-ho," the mistress trilled, shedding bonnet and cape and hastening towards the fire to warm herself. "Such a to-do at the manor today, Holly. We were sitting in the parlour talking when suddenly there was such an almighty rumpus below stairs." She giggled girlishly. "It set our hostess's little dogs yapping and one of the ladies spilled her tea in fright!"

"Whatever had happened?"

"Apparently one of the new young maids dropped a mixing bowl of the pot-pourri intended for the guest rooms and smashed it. There was broken china and flower-bits everywhere.

"The whole mixture was ruined," the mistress continued, with a grimace of sympathy, "because most of it fell into a bucket of water — it was waiting for the scullery floor to be scrubbed.

"Such a noise we could hear — the still-room maid lamenting, the younger girl wailing because she'd had her ears boxed! You've never heard the like!"

Holly could well imagine the situation. All that time and effort — gone! She had been in service long enough to know how vital these niceties were in the general order of things. Guests in the house over the festive season, the place decorated — and to have no pretty dishes of petals to scent the air!

"You may go, Holly. I shan't need you till later," the mistress said, yawning delicately behind her hand. "I'm just going to have a little nap now."

Holly dipped a curtsey and withdrew. Her mind churned. She had more pot-pourri than she could cope with and she was a firm believer in all things being meant.

If she left the crock outside the garden gate, chances were Jake would find it. Jake would know what to do.

*   *   *   *

Fetching the crock from her room, Holly threw on her shawl and went out into the darkening day.

As she hurried through the woods, thick snowflakes fell, sticking to her eyelashes, blurring her vision. Rounding a bend in the path, she all but cannoned into another traveller who was approaching at speed, his coat collar pulled up round his ears.

"Oh!" she yelped, startled.

"Holly! I was on my way to see you."

It was Jake and as he turned down his collar, Holly's heart gave a little flip when she saw how he was smiling at her.

"Was it about the pot-pourri?" she asked. "I heard what had happened at the manor. I've made more than enough for my purposes, so I thought they might be glad of this."

"Well then, that's very thoughtful of you, Holly," Jake said. "That — that wasn't that I've come about, though. I wanted to ask you something."

Jake shuffled his feet, suddenly shy and awkward.

"I wondered if you'd come with me to the Yuletide Supper?"

Holly's heart leaped.

"Oh, Jake, I'd love to come!"

"That's grand news." Jake beamed at her. "I wasn't sure how you'd be about it. I . . . I mean, you'd stopped leaving those treats . . ."

"I know." Holly hesitated, thankful that the cold had already coloured her cheeks — perhaps he wouldn't notice her blush! "I thought you'd think me forward . . . or just plain silly."

"Never that. I don't know, Holly, it's been a pickle of a time. I was offered a job at the manor — a permanent one."

"Instead of going as a journeyman, like you said? Have you accepted it?"

"Not yet. A few weeks ago I'd have turned it down there and then. But you had come into the picture . . . and I couldn't seem to think straight any more."

"Because of me?" Holly could hardly believe what he was saying.

"Because I felt I wanted to know you better."

"Same with me, Jake," Holly admitted softly.

"Is that so?" Jake's voice rose in delighted surprise. "Holly, would you be my girl?"

Holly gazed up at him, the snowflakes drifting soundlessly around them. Her heart was beating so loudly she felt he must surely hear it.

She didn't want to shatter this most perfect of moments, but some instinct deep within her advised caution.

"I'd be proud to walk out with you, Jake," she said solemnly. "But I'll not hold you back. If your heart's still set on being a journeyman, I can understand. You've got to make your way in life and we can still keep in touch, can't we? Don't you feel obliged to stop on at the manor because of me."

IT cost Holly a great deal to say the words, and yet it was heartening to see the sweet smile of pride and appreciation that spread over Jake's face.

"You're sure? It'll be worth our while, I promise. A gardener with some experience under his belt gets a choice of all the best houses — and a decent cottage to start wedded life in, too."

He traced a gentle fingertip across her cheek.

"My Holly. Suits you, that name. Not likely to forget when it was we met, are we?"

"Not at all. Mam called me that because I was born when the berries ripened. Oh, Jake, what a lot we've to learn about each other." She smiled up at him. "It'll be such fun. Think of the good times ahead."

"Starting with that Yuletide Supper!" Jake tucked the crock of pot-pourri under one arm and took her hand in his. "Come on, it's getting dark. Let me walk you back . . ."

Behind them, beyond the high wall, the garden drowsed under the sifting mantle of snow. Above, the Christmas star gleamed down through the lacing branches.

"Look, the star's shining especially for us," Jake said. "Happy Christmas, Holly."

"Happy Christmas, Jake," she replied.

And it was. ■

Printed and Published in Great Britain by D.C. Thomson & Co., Ltd., Dundee, Glasgow and London.

ISBN 978 1 84535 391 9
EAN 9 781845 353919

Ardrossan, North Ayrshire, Scotland

*T*HANK you so much for the beautiful picture of Ardrossan that you had on the cover of the "Friend". My family actually lived in this seaside town for a short time and I went to primary school there. I still have relatives there, or just down the road in Saltcoats or